After S
and othe

ABOUT WRITING WEST MIDLANDS

Writing West Midlands is the literature development agency for the West Midlands region of the UK. We run events and activities for writers and readers, including our annual Birmingham Literature Festival. We also run Spark Young Writers, which is a major programme of work for young writers aged 8 to 16+ including regular workshops, a summer

school and a magazine. Writing West Midlands also works with libraries, publishers and universities to help creative writers develop their skills.

ABOUT READ ON!

READ ON! is a major Creative Europe funded project across six European countries working in five languages. It aims to encourage young people aged 12 to 19 to engage with reading and creative writing. Writing West Midlands is the UK partner. Work taking place in the West Midlands includes creative writing workshops, a young presenters scheme as part of the Birmingham Literature Festival and training sessions on vlogging and podcasting. The *After Summer* anthology has been produced as part of READ ON!

AFTER SUMMER

&

Other Stories

THE EMMA PRESS

ACKNOWLEDGEMENTS

'The Headstrong Historian' by Chimamanda Ngozi
Adichie is reprinted by permission of Harper Collins
Publisher Ltd. © 2009 Chimamanda Ngozi Adichie

'Getting the Messages' by Anne Fine, from *Very
Different and Other Stories* (Mammoth, 2001), reproduced
by permission of David Higham Associates Limited.

Co-funded by the
Creative Europe Programme
of the European Union

Contents

After Summer
Emma Purshouse

I had a good start, I don't deny it. Mum's a famous fashion designer. You've probably heard of her. Dad, a business man. They're... well... rich. What more can I say? That's how they've been able to pay for so much therapy. Therapy has been the thing ever since I started seeing the dead.

It began at our old house. I say house, it was more of a mansion really.

It... she... the first one... was a small blue-faced thing, dirty clothes, long matted dark hair. She scuttled along the top corridor one day, disappeared through a wall, leaving nothing but the faint smell of oranges.

You tell them about the first few, of course, because you don't know any better. You don't realise that they, your parents, can't see them. At first they laughed. *Imaginary friends*, they said, *how sweet.*

Janey was harmless enough, I suppose. Cartwheeling and doing handstands around the garden, annoying like a kid sister might be. She had three pets that used to appear with her. Hogle was full black with green eyes, Jarth similar but with a spot of white, and Jess. *My Jess is white with white spots,* the kid would giggle. Same joke every time. Dull after a bit.

Yeah, I suppose some of the dead were scary. Although I think it was my parents who found it more freaky. Their disgust was evident. My 'stories' developed as I tuned in more effectively and described every foot-sniffing, toe-licking creature of the night that was creeping about the house, dragging their stitched-up, ripped-up bodies over the creaking floorboards, and knock-knock-knocking at our bedroom doors.

As I got older I learned to stop mentioning them so much. I also learned how to put them out of their misery... the ghosts, the shades, the spooks... whatever you like to call them. I was quite happy to believe the hype, the spreading of hate by Mum and Dad, the stuff on the TV. *The dead are all evil! The dead devalue our properties!* The Facebook rants and the anti-dead social media pages all played their part in colouring my beliefs. I thought I'd do my bit. I could see them, made sense that I should help the cause. I did my research. Read a few books on eradication, then there was Google, Wikipedia, that sort of thing.

I learned the hard way that holy water doesn't work. That's how I got this scar by my eye. And don't believe what they tell you about the dead not having a punch on them. Little Janey and her pets went down fighting. Like I say she was annoying, and I had to hone my skills somehow. Guilty? I suppose... for a little while. Although, when they come back at you scratching and biting, you soon lose sympathy.

One of the last ones tried to rag my hair out by the roots in the final showdown. That's why I went short. The purple tips were a nice touch I thought. Yes, I know, the combat trousers and heavy duty para boots were a bit OTT, but it's sort of what people expected from a ghost hunter.

That's what I was. Much to the annoyance of the parents. They thought I'd let them down, that it wasn't an appropriate profession. Hey, I was just being entrepreneurial. Like them, I was making the most of my skills. They set me up with a little place to keep me out of their way, and they were still paying for the therapy.

My last therapist asked me weird questions. *Isella, what's the most beautiful thing you've ever seen?*

A deer, I told her, *in the woodland at the back of Dad's place*. Did I mention my parents are divorced now? No? Well, they are. The therapist looked pleased at my answer. I didn't tell her it was a dead deer. But it was. I could see the bullet hole in its side as it grazed on oblivious, cropping at its ghost grass.

I was actually on my way back from the therapist's office when I first saw the girl.

Look, there she is. Do you see her? Well, perhaps you don't have the sight. That one there... who looks like she isn't afraid of anything, the one who looks capable of murder. She's just lifted that bag of shopping from by the feet of that old man in the bus queue. He hasn't even noticed.

I wondered if she was one of the spooks they'd called me about from the Royal Hospital... the old building, where the developers were. One of the site workmen had called it in. You're supposed to report sightings direct to the authorities, like when you get bats in a building. It's ridiculous though, results in automatic preservation orders, so things can't just be knocked down. Contractors want them all gone on the quiet. The bats. And the dead. There are pest exterminators who'll do the bats for a bit of cash in hand. And there are people like me to take out the dead. Like this one, this girl with the red hair.

See her yet? Her pale face turning to scan the street as she melts into that doorway. Most people could see if they wanted to, but they turn a blind eye. Tune in. Go on. Look at her ripped clothes. She's small, skinny even. She's standing behind the grimy sleeping bag somebody has dumped there.

When I reached into my back pocket for my iPhone, to check the listings they'd sent me for a match, it had vanished. Damn! I never felt it go. I narrowed my eyes and studied her harder, started to walk towards her. She was going through the bag she'd lifted. *Hah, dog food!* she muttered, with a suck of her ghost teeth. Then she inspected her phone... my phone.

You cheeky... I made a move forward. *That's mine you little bi...* She looked at me straight.

How the hell can you see me, freak? she said, *I'm dead to the world. Nobody notices me.*

I must've looked shocked. They don't know usually. No clue that they've gone. I looked for an indication of whatever saw her off. Nothing visible. No half-caved-in head or anything. I was still gawping when she ran, taking the bag of shopping with her. And my damn phone.

They still think they need to eat... the dead. Force of habit I suppose. But this one seemed to think she needed to make phone calls too. I legged it after her. Up and across the car park. She was straight out onto the dual carriageway, crossing the two lanes of traffic. Nobody seemed to see her... nothing swerved or stopped. Waiting for the green man, I was too slow. I watched her scrabble through a gap between the wood panels that they'd put up around the hospital, and then disappear under the *keep out, danger demolition in progress* sign. I'd lost her.

When I got home I plugged myself into the broadband, checked my emails. And there she was. Five or six reported sightings. A flash of red hair there. A glimpse of a skinny girl here. The other reports were of strange smells, a sort of medicinal burning sensation in the backs of throats. Some of it would be their overactive imaginations of course. But some of it... well, we'd see.

As I climbed in through the broken window the book was on the sill.

My name is... was Summer. I was loved once but now I'm lost. You should always tell your family you love them because you never know when you might see them again. Tonight I've eaten dog food for the first time. It isn't as bad as I thought it might be.

A journal of sorts, open at the last entry. Had she been hiding here? Had she tripped and fallen down a flight of stairs?

I flicked through the earlier pages, not reading as such, more registering that it was full of even but slightly sloping writing. I wondered if she was watching me as I read.

My attention was taken by a halo of light above my head. One of those things that sometimes appear on photos... a sort of half-hearted circle of photons. The psychics call them orbs. I gave it a jet of Mr Muscle taken from the holster at my belt and it vanished. I know, please don't tell anyone, but it works. Holy water, no. Bathroom cleaner from Poundland, yes. I don't make the rules.

I set to. Scoped out the place. Methodical. Checked each room in turn. For bodies and ghosts. First floor, second floor, third floor. Every cupboard, nook, cranny. I got a faint waft of one of the medicinal smells as described in the email. But it was an old hospital for god's sake, what would they expect it to smell of. I took down another couple of orbs. Sprayed Mr Muscle into corners as a precaution. The building felt unstable. It creaked and groaned. I returned to where I'd started, pretty sure that the place was now clear of spooks.

I guess the room I was in must have been some sort of entrance hall. It was grand... or at least it had been grand. I'd done a little extra research the previous night, which showed that the hospital had opened in Victorian times and closed in 1972. The Victorians knew how to build. I patrolled the edges of the room. Nothing left of what it was. No medical things. All stripped out. Well, unless you were to count the syringes on the floor, but they were new. Glass crunched under my boots as I moved around in the half-light. It smelt skunky in there. A taste in the air of old money and metal. There were stains on the floors which might have been blood... but more likely paint. There were dark corners, scratch marks on the walls. It was easy to imagine the screams of lunatics, and mad women. There was some evidence it had been used as an asylum. It was the kind of place adventurous kids might want to explore. There was another waft of something medicinal.

And then it came. Screaming out of the wall at me. Teeth and clawing hands, spittle flying from its jaws. What in hell's name? It slammed into me and I was on the floor. My Mr Muscle went flying. My rucksack was still on my back. No weapons at my disposal. Nothing. Its breath was stultifying, I felt the vomit rise up in my throat. Bone-hard fingers dug themselves in either side of my windpipe. I couldn't have screamed even if I'd wanted to. Its red eyes blinked, its mouth opened and its needle teeth closed in towards my face. And just as I was giving up hope... just as the darkness came for me... the thing turned its head... distracted for a second. I managed to get my foot up under it, and kick in with my boot to where I imagined its solar plexus to be. AAAAGGHHHGHH!!! The exertion was immense. And the creature's scream was immense... like nothing on earth... like all the sorrows, deaths and tortures of this place had joined together in one mass of noise. It vaporised. Disappeared... for the time being. I could hear it moaning somewhere in the walls.

I was lying on my back trying to get my breath, when I saw her staring at me. I realised then it must have been her sudden appearance that had distracted it... the thing. *What the hell was that?* I mumbled. Sitting up, I shrugged my rucksack off. I was taking no chances. I pulled out weapons, books of summoning, laser pens, Tasers, the high frequency oscillator. I lined up my arsenal on the floor.

You read my diary! she said, quietly.

What?

You read my diary! she repeated.

Only a bit. The last page. She nodded. Looked at me uncertain. *And then I stopped. When that thing came flying out of the...*

You epileptic? she said.

What? I said again. I'm not really used to the third degree from ghosts.

When I came in you looked like you were having a fit or something.

Well, fending off rabid, frothing at the mouth, dead things can do that do you?

8

She looked confused again. *You know the spawn of Satan... needle teeth...* And then I realised... she hadn't seen it. How could she have not seen it? They can all see each other.

What's with the things? She pointed at the bits and pieces on the floor by my rucksack. I felt embarrassed about the Mr Muscle and retrieved it from where it had fallen, put it back in my holster.

Errr... it's my ghost zapping kit. She was weirding me out. I don't ever talk to them.

Have you come to exorcise me? She smiled, then. I smiled back in spite of myself.

Well, that was the plan. But seems there are bigger fish to fry. A moan leaked out of the wall. *Did you hear that?* She shook her head.

They want to build here. Maybe it's the builders coming back?

The moaning increased. *Nope, that wasn't a builder.* A groan. And then there it was again. The stench, the wall shimmering and the demonic presence, all needles and claws. It came screaming at me, passing straight through Summer as she stood there unmoving. I was ready. I rolled sideways, grabbed a Taser and gave it a thousand volts. The shriek was palpable and burnt the air. Still not enough. It came at me again. *Grab the book.* I shouted at Summer. I rolled over to my right as the thing bore down on me. *The book... page 22... Read it backwards.* She reacted then. I realised all she had to go on was me thrashing about on the floor screaming instructions about how

9

to eradicate a demon she couldn't even see. But she did it... she did it. She read the summoning backwards. As is the best way of dealing with an Amorphus. And as she finished, I let fly with a Taser again, and somewhere between us we managed to rid the hospital of one of its ghosts. The bang was quite something. Summer didn't even flinch. How the hell couldn't she hear that?

You can't stop here. I said, after we'd both got our breath back. *You saved my life. I owe you, and I won't eradicate you now... unless you want to be eradicated that is,* I added as an afterthought.

I'm not sure... I...

Whatever, but you can't stop here.

Oi, Summer! A voice from outside broke up our conversation. *Where are ya? I know you're in there... Don't make me look for you. Cuz when I find you, bab...* Summer clearly heard this one. She was up on her feet before I could speak and she ran, scrambled out of the window, and was gone.

I leapt up. *Summer...* I shouted, following after her. When I got out into the sunshine there was no sign of her.

I was exhausted, and decided I didn't want any more ghost trouble that day. Summer and the owner of the voice would have to wait until tomorrow. I'd previously had no qualms about ridding the world of the dead... Well, you know, they're dead so it's not really an issue to send them off to the next world... or oblivion... or wherever it is the dead go. I'd not really thought about where they go. It's not like they matter though, is it? But still, that night

I started to feel awkward about her. Well, for one we'd sort of got on. And she had saved my life. The needle-jawed creature wasn't taking any prisoners. And there was another thing. I was intrigued, I suppose. Why couldn't she see the demon?

I did a bit of admin. Logged the orbs, the needle-jawed medicinal smell problem and let the company know they'd been neutralised. I hadn't been aware of anything else obvious, but where there is one orb there are often others, like cockroaches. I decided to go back the next day and sort that out, check on the owner of that voice, and then try, if she was still there, to convince Summer to move on.

The dead aren't tied to a place. Though they sometimes think they are. Often they haunt where they died, but sometimes they stay where they were happy. But if they want to, they can go somewhere else. She... it... probably just needed a bit of gentle persuasion. And if not... well there was always the Taser. I hoped it wouldn't come to that. I really needed to unwind, so I stuck some cartoons on, binge-watched some Netflix. Finally got to sleep about 2am.

I woke again with a start at about 4, replaying the bit where old Needle Jaws had gone *Boom!* and Summer and I had both stood getting our breath back. *Damn it, of course!*

I was eating breakfast when the company called with reports of lights being seen in the old hospital building that night. A couple of members of the public had called it in this time. That wasn't good. Sometimes when the public get wind of a haunting you get the do-gooders wanting to 'save the dead'. Protests and banner-waving mean building demolitions and renovations massively held up. And then I'd be getting a bad press. I couldn't have that.

I checked my weapons, and set off. When I reached the hospital I got through the same window I'd gone in through the day before. The orbs were probably all gone, but I put some more Mr Muscle into the cobwebs to be safe.

Her book was still there on the sill. I read an earlier entry.

I thought I saw him in the town. It can't be him though. I'm just seeing things. I'm a long way from home. He wouldn't find me here. Nobody knows me here. But it looked like him. My skin crawled, and I felt sick inside like I do when I see him. But I know my imagination is playing tricks. A panic attack or something. I managed to lift some bananas off the market. They'll keep me going I suppose. I don't even like bananas ☺

As I was reading, there was a scream. I knew it then, I was right. A scream like that, only one explanation. I ran to the bottom of the main stairs. I was up them two at a time. Another scream. *Get away from me!* I heard her cry.

I skidded out onto the first floor landing. Ran to the doorways of each of the old wards in turn, and looked in each one. In the last but one I found her, a huge shape standing over her. The creature had its back to me. Its laughter chilled me. I ditched the rucksack off my back, knelt to open it. It must have seen her look towards me. It turned then, the abomination.

Who's this, then? You got a little friend, Summer? It walked towards me. And I let him have it, a dose of sound from the ultrasonic oscillator, which by rights should have burst his ghostly eardrums. Nothing. He kept moving towards me, then made a lunge. I dodged him. He made another, grabbed at my T-shirt. I ripped myself from his grasp, looked round the room. A piece of wood in the corner. I snatched it up, lashed out as he went for me again. Vibrations jarred through me as I smacked it down onto his head. He put his hand to his skull, and then he started bleeding. Bleeding!?! He staggered a bit, but was still coming for me... still laughing. He was so much bigger than me. And he was flesh and blood and bone! That was not good. Not good at all. The punch he threw rattled my jaw, knocked me sideways to the wall. I could see that Summer was up on her feet now. At least I'd distracted him enough for her to get her wits about her. Two against one. Unless she ran. I wouldn't blame her if she ran. But she didn't. She leapt then. Onto his back. Screaming fit to shake the walls down. Smashing her small fists into his head. He spun round and round trying to shake her off. I watched, not sure what to do. I moved round the room to the side of them. The floor creaked under my feet, the boards gave way under my foot, sending rotting wood and plasterboard down into the hall below. I leapt to the wall at the room's edge.

Come and get me! I shouted. And he lunged, bringing Summer with him. Her legs were wrapped around his waist, her eyes shut, her fists still smacking his head. He lumbered towards the small hole where my foot had passed through the ceiling. He was big. His weight and

Summer's added weight created more splintering. His right leg disappeared into the hole, pitching him to the side. *Summer, let him go!* She looked like she couldn't hear, like she'd gone somewhere else. *Give me your hand!* Her eyes were wild as if she didn't recognise me. *Your hand, Summer!* He tried to pull himself back up through the hole. *Summer! Your hand!* She reached for me. And as she let go and made a grab for my arm, I pulled her free of him. A well-judged para boot connected with his face as he tried again to heave himself up from the gaping mouth of the floor, but the boards were too rotten. He crashed through the ceiling, with a weird dog-like yelp. The thud on the floor below was hard... but inconclusive.

Summer, come on! We ran from the room as more of the ceiling caved. We hurtled down the stairs to find his body lying there. *You've killed him,* she whispered.

Yeah, well... I suddenly didn't know what to say. It's one thing killing the dead, but the living...

The mist started to rise. I grabbed the Taser and gave his spirit what for. Bang. He/it was gone.

Jeez, that was mad. I said. There was no answer. I turned to see Summer climbing through the window. *You're not dead, Summer!* I shouted. She turned for a second. *You can't see the dead, and when we fought off the demon you had to stop to get your breath. The dead don't breathe. You're not dead.*

I might as well be, she said. She smiled with her mouth but not her eyes. And then I did see her pain, her wounds

14

clearer as she lifted her hand and gave me a sad sort of a wave as she left. I wondered how long she'd got left. How long it would be before I saw her again. Next time I knew I wouldn't let her go.

• • •

'After Summer' was commissioned by the young writers of Balaam Wood School, Birmingham: **Mohamed, Jessica, Hayleigh, Amber, Jack, Christopher, Roman, Jackson, Rynae, Dyllan, Kelis, Leah, Bradley, Josh** and **Allyra**.
Teacher: **Emma Turrell.**

ABOUT THE AUTHOR

Emma Purshouse was born in Wolverhampton and is a freelance writer and performance poet. She is a poetry slam champion and performs regularly at spoken word nights and festivals far and wide, often using her native Black Country dialect in her work. She writes for both children and adults.

Emma's first collection of children's poetry was published by Fair Acre Press in 2016 and won the poetry section of the Rubery Book Award. Her most recent publication is *Close* (Offa's Press, 2018).

EMMA SAYS:

'When I was asked to write a story with and for a small group of students, I was excited. I arrived at the school to find out I'd be working with over twenty Year 7s who were keen to have their ideas on settings, character creation and plot twists incorporated into a short story of a genre which they had chosen. And that's how I ended up writing a horror/adventure story. It certainly isn't a style of writing I'd naturally gravitate towards, but it was good fun trying to include all of their ideas and descriptions which had come out of the workshop I'd run.

A couple of weeks later I returned to the school with a draft story which I hoped each and every participant would feel able to recognise something of their own contribution in. We read through the piece together and the students made one or two suggestions for changes which I acted on.

It was certainly an interesting process, and I loved talking to the young people about the sort of films they watched and books that they read. I hope they enjoy the end result.'

FallDeep

Ken Preston

Lucy pulled the trigger on the shotgun and the dreadite exploded in a shower of guts and flesh and bone. Quickly ejecting the two spent shells, she then slid two more in the chamber and pumped the shotgun to prime it.

'This way!' Mr Digits shouted, leaping over a porter's cage and scampering down the hospital corridor. He screeched with delight and performed a couple of somersaults as he ran. The others followed the chimpanzee as he led them to safety.

Lucy remained standing right where she was, shotgun aimed at the advancing dreadites.

The dreadites were an unholy combination of human and spider. Their humanoid bodies were held aloft by the long, thin spindly legs that had erupted from their torsos. Their bodies were covered in dark brown bristles, and their eyes glowed red with hunger and hate. If a dreadite managed to pin you to the floor with its six legs, it then lowered itself until it was close enough that it could start eating you.

The nearest dreadite opened its mouth to reveal rows of sharp, pointed fangs dripping saliva. Each drop of saliva sizzled and steamed and burnt a hole in the floor.

Lucy squeezed the trigger and let loose another explosion of shrapnel. The blast blew a hole right through the dreadite's stomach. For a moment it simply stood there, almost looking surprised, and then it collapsed to the floor, legs splayed out everywhere.

More of the monsters gathered behind the corpse and stared balefully at Lucy.

Lucy reached for more shotgun pellets.

None left.

She'd run out.

Lucy turned and ran.

She followed the children down the hospital corridor. Strip lights flickered on and off, casting weird shadows over the walls. Lucy couldn't see the children, but she could hear them. Some of them were screaming, and some laughing. The ones laughing still thought this was just a game. That if they got eaten by a dreadite, they would be thrown out of the game and given the option of starting again, or leaving FallDeep entirely.

That was the way it used to be, but staying alive in Fall-Deep was no game anymore.

It was deadly reality.

No one was sure what had happened, or when. FallDeep was the largest, most immersive virtual environment ever created. Some players had spent years exploring and mapping it out, and still not approached its edges. No one knew how far and wide FallDeep extended, and the creators weren't telling.

Lucy had only explored a tiny part, spending most of her time running missions with her friends Aurora and Alex, in the technologically advanced city of Deepopolis. The skyscrapers were impossibly tall and beautiful, and the city hummed with vibrant, multicultural, interplanetary life.

Lucy knew that none of the citizens of FallDeep were real, even as she wasn't real. They were avatars, made of little more than pixels and the personalities of the players behind the pixels. That was the beautiful thing about FallDeep. People came here to be who they wanted to be, and you could be absolutely anyone or anything. There were no barriers, no distinctions between race or gender or sexuality.

Many players came to FallDeep to simply enjoy the place itself, to soak it up and live here like it was reality. Lucy knew players who had met other players and got married, or started a family together. They had got jobs, bought places to live, gone exploring outside of the city or taken holidays to other countries.

Still others had made it their mission to explore Fall-Deep, crossing oceans and mountains and exploring further and deeper than anyone else. Many of these players worked and lived alone, content in their own company.

FallDeep wasn't a game.

It was life.

But real life outside of the virtual environment remained. Even the hardiest of players had to leave and return to reality even if just to feed themselves.

Except now, everyone was trapped in FallDeep.

It had started with avatars dying but not returning. Avatars dying in FallDeep was a fairly common occurrence, but players soon came back with more lives. But then they stopped returning. In her last communication with her best friend Alex before contact with the real world was shut down, Lucy had found out that anyone who left the game, died.

They were trapped.

Lucy ran through a set of double doors and turned to close them. Mr Digits was waiting for her and together they barricaded the door shut.

Mr Digits rolled on his back and shrieked with laughter. He was excitable like that.

'I'm glad you find this funny,' Lucy said.

'I can't help it,' the chimpanzee said. 'This is the most fun I've had since I stopped working in the movies.'

You never were in the movies, Lucy thought, but kept her mouth shut. Mr Digits was part of the virtual environment of FallDeep. He wasn't a player's avatar; no one controlled him. When the dreadites had begun hunting them, Mr Digits had chosen to help Lucy and her companions.

Lucy wasn't sure how much help he actually was, but she was grateful to have him around.

Even if he had an unpleasant habit of sticking his finger up his nose and having a good root around until he found something nice and juicy to eat.

Lucy looked at the boarded up doors.

'It's not going to hold them for long,' she said.

'Hot diggity dog, we'd better vamoose,' Mr Digits said.

One of the older children appeared from the gloom behind them.

'There's nowhere to go,' he said. 'It's a dead end.'

The boarded up doors trembled beneath a pounding and battering.

'Holy shmoly,' Mr Digits said. 'Looks like we're for the big chop.'

Lucy closed her eyes. This was it then.

If only Aurora and Alex were here. They would know what to do.

But Alex had not been in FallDeep when the crisis hit.

And no one had seen Aurora for a long, long time.

'**W**orldwide it is estimated that there are over nine million players stuck inside FallDeep. And the number of players who have died either trying to exit the game or through death in the game now stands at over twenty-five thousand. We are seeing international cooperation on a scale never imagined before as specialists come together to find a way of rescuing the remaining players from the game. But it will not be easy.'

Alex flicked the news off. He was sick of it, sick of the constant coverage, the never ending commentary even when there was no fresh news to report.

And he was worried about Lucy.

Alex was in constant touch with Lucy's parents, who were sitting beside their daughter as she lay in her gaming chair, her VR helmet and gloves on. She was alive, and active within FallDeep, they knew that much. But nothing else. The FallDeep crisis was approaching the twelve hour mark and discussions were ongoing about how best to look after the players' physical needs whilst they were still trapped in the game. Solutions so far included fitting drip feeds to keep the players hydrated and catheters to take care of body waste.

His frustration and worry mounting, Alex looked at his own VR kit. Not for the first time he wished the game wasn't in lockdown so he could go to FallDeep and find Lucy.

TED, the house AI, interrupted Alex's thoughts.

'You have a call, Alex.'

Alex climbed into his gaming chair and slipped the VR helmet and his sensory gloves on.

He navigated to the chat room, walking in to a cafe on a New York street corner. As always, whenever he first entered the VR world, it astonished him how real everything looked and felt. The yellow taxis rumbling by outside the cafe windows, the barista waiting to take orders at the counter, the hum of conversation from people sat around tables.

Alex's caller was the man standing by the counter. He wore a suit and a hat, looking like one of those private eyes from the old films that Alex's dad watched, and sometimes forced on Alex.

'Good afternoon, Alex,' the man said.

As he spoke his ID appeared, hovering beside the man's right shoulder.

Government Agent Brett Gideon, Special Consultant for the FallDeep Taskforce.

'I'll come straight to the point,' Agent Gideon said. 'We're assembling as many teams as we can to go into FallDeep and rescue the players stuck there. As you can –'

'You've found a way in?' Alex said, his excitement mounting.

Agent Gideon nodded, his face grim. 'Yes, we've found a way in. But it's not an easy way. Alex, do you have any experience with forcejumping?'

'No,' Alex said.

Forcejumping was a means of travelling quickly from one point in FallDeep to another. Players could navigate thousands of miles in only a minute or two by taking a series of virtual 'shortcuts'. But it took many months of training to master the skills needed, and not everyone succeeded.

'No, I thought not,' Agent Gideon said. 'But you know someone who does, right?'

'You mean Aurora?' Alex said. 'Aurora hasn't been in FallDeep for at least a couple of months now. No one knows where she is, or who she is.'

'We do,' Agent Gideon said. 'We've already been in touch and she's willing to go into FallDeep one last time, but only if you go with her.'

The traffic noise grew louder as the cafe door opened.

Aurora strode inside and said, 'Hi Alex. You ready for some action?'

For a second, Alex was lost for words. Aurora, Lucy and Alex had been a team once, a trio who shared everything within FallDeep and travelled together everywhere, sharing adventures, experiences and many conversations within the city of Deepopolis or out camping, sitting around a campfire into the night. Neither Alex nor Lucy knew Aurora in the real world, but their friendship was as strong as anyone's.

And then Aurora had gone, with no explanation.

Now, with Aurora standing in front of him, that grin playing across her lips and those deep blue eyes focused steadily upon him, Alex didn't know whether to be happy or angry.

In the end, Aurora spoke for him.

'Come on, let's get moving. We need to rescue Lucy.'

Agent Gideon took them through to the back of the cafe and down to a steep flight of stairs to the basement. There was a plain wooden door set in the basement wall.

'We've managed to open up a series of portals into Fall-Deep all around the world. There are teams going in as we speak, thousands of them. Once you're in, there's no guarantee you will be able to find your way back again. No one's forcing you to go, this is your decision. But you have to make it now. We can't keep these portals open for long.'

Alex looked at Aurora and grinned. Despite the danger, the old excitement was coming back.

'I'm ready,' Alex said. 'What about you?'

'I was born ready,' Aurora said.

Alex's grin widened.

Aurora was back, for sure.

Agent Gideon pulled an old-fashioned mortice key from a pocket. He placed the key in the lock and turned it.

He stood back.

'Good luck,' he said. 'Come back, and bring some friends with you.'

Aurora nodded at Agent Gideon, opened the door and stepped through it.

Alex followed her.

The air was freezing on the other side and a fierce wind buffeted them with whirling, sharp-edged snowflakes. Alex heard the door slam shut behind him.

Alex grabbed Aurora when he realised they were perched on the icy spine of a mountain range. He looked back to see the plain, wooden door hovering inches above the top of the mountain.

'Where are we?' Alex yelled.

'HighDeep!' Aurora shouted back, the wind snatching her words away so that Alex only just heard her. 'Come on, we need to climb down to find the next door.'

They followed a steep, narrow icy path down the side of the mountain. The wind brought tears to Alex's eyes, and the cold froze them to his cheeks. There were so many questions he had for Aurora, not least of which was where she had been all this time, and why. But the howling wind made talking impossible.

The path twisted and turned through the rocky landscape of ice and snow.

Suddenly it opened out, and they were confronted by three men in white snow outfits, goggles and helmets.

And they had guns.

'Kcurt ehtni teg!' one of the men shouted, waving his gun at the two teenagers.

He pointed at a battered lorry parked behind them.

Alex's heart sank.

'What do we do?' he whispered to Aurora.

'Get in the lorry,' Aurora said.

They walked over to it, hands up and heads down against the freezing wind. They climbed inside and the man slammed the door shut and locked it. A moment later the engine started up.

Alex put his head in his hands as they jerked into

movement. Soon they had picked up speed, rattling and bouncing over the rocky ground.

'I can't believe it,' Alex said. 'We've failed even before we got started.'

'No, we haven't,' Aurora said.

Alex looked up.

Aurora had pulled open a trapdoor in the lorry's floor. Alex crawled over and looked through the square doorway.

Instead of the icy, rocky path speeding by, as Alex had expected to see, there was green, moss covered ground.

And it was perfectly still.

'Quick,' Aurora said, 'before the portal closes.'

Alex swung his legs over and dropped feet first through the hole, landing on soft ground. He rolled out of the way and Aurora landed beside him. Alex sat up and looked at his surroundings.

They were in a dense forest. The air was thick with the smell of vegetation. Moisture dripped from the trees and ran down the thick, green trunks.

Alex pointed at the trees.

'Wait a second, is that, are they –'

'Broccoli, yes,' Aurora said. 'We're in a forest of giant broccoli.'

Alex shook his head. These were parts of FallDeep he had never even heard of.

'Right, let's get moving, we need to find the next doorway,' Aurora said. 'I haven't got much time.'

'You mean, we haven't got much time,' Alex said.

'That's what I said,' Aurora replied and strode off.

Something's wrong, Alex thought. He didn't know what, but something about Aurora was different.

The next door was embedded in the trunk of a broccoli tree. Aurora opened the doorway, and they both stepped through.

'Ouch!' Alex yelled as he banged his head on a low ceiling, producing a metallic clanging noise.

They were in a submarine. The crew turned to look at the newcomers.

The crew were all female, almost identical with their long, black hair and insect-like feelers protruding from their foreheads. And they were short, too. Alex had to bend to keep from banging his head on the submarine's low ceiling.

They looked at Alex and Aurora, wide-eyed with surprise.

Aurora grasped the metal handle on another door and turned to Alex. 'One more door after this one and we will be right where Lucy is, but you need to be careful in this next section.'

'Why? What are you talking about?' Alex said.

Aurora opened the door and stepped through, calling back to Alex, 'Because the creatures in here bite!'

'Great,' Alex muttered, as he stepped through the doorway.

Mr Digits leapt up and down, chattering and squealing with laughter.

The children, about fifty of them all together, huddled at the far end of the deserted hospital ward, silent and withdrawn.

The barricaded doors shuddered beneath the onslaught of the dreadites. Already holes had appeared in the doors where the dreadites' saliva was burning its way through. Lucy didn't think they had much longer.

Mr Digits somersaulted in front of Lucy and scratched his backside. 'Wow! This is fun, right?'

'No,' Lucy said, close to tears. 'Any moment now those doors will give way and the dreadites will charge in here and kill us.'

Mr Digits stood up on his legs and thrust his hairy chest out, beating it with his fists. 'Don't worry kid, I won't let that happen. I'll protect you!'

Lucy smiled weakly.

Mr Digits had been a loyal and brave companion, sacrificing himself several times over whilst protecting Lucy and the others. Because he was a part of the game, and not a player, he always came back to life after a few moments. But no matter how often he returned, the dreadites always advanced, and now they were trapped. Lucy had checked the ward windows, but they were too high to jump from and there were more dreadites waiting for them on the ground.

The doors crashed open. Dreadites scrambled through the doorway and over the wreckage, hungry for human flesh.

Mr Digits jumped in front of Lucy and the children and stood tall, spreading his arms out.

'Stay back, you filthy animals, you're not getting past me!' he roared.

The nearest dreadite bent down, picked Mr Digits up and sank its teeth into his neck. Lucy covered her ears as the chimp screamed.

The dreadite chomped on Mr Digits until the screaming stopped, and then casually threw the chimp's body aside.

Blood and saliva dripped from its jaws as it scuttled closer on its spindly legs.

More dreadites pushed in behind it.

Lucy stood her ground, the children behind her screaming and crying. She held out her arms, much like Mr Digits had done only moments before, in an effort to protect the children for as long as she could.

The dreadite that had killed Mr Digits leaned in close. Lucy could feel its hot, stinking breath on her face, and she could hear the sizzle of its saliva as each drop hit the floor.

She screwed her eyes shut, waiting for its savage bite.

A gunshot rang out.

Lucy opened her eyes just as the dreadite's head exploded in a shower of blood and brains, splattering Lucy's hair and face.

'Alex! Aurora!' she yelled.

The two teenagers waded through the army of dreadites, firing their guns and sending the long-legged monstrosities flying. The children cheered.

Alex and Aurora seemed to have an endless supply of ammunition. They waded into the pack of dreadites, their guns blazing. It was only minutes before the walls were dripping with dreadite blood, and the monsters were lying dead in pools of flesh and bone.

Lucy ran and hugged Alex and then Aurora.

'How did you get here?' she said.

'You wouldn't believe it,' Alex replied, wiping an arm across his forehead. 'But it was Aurora, she did it all.'

'Have you come to rescue us? Can you get us out?'

'I don't know, I hope so. First thing we have to do is get out of this place before we're attacked by more dreadites.'

'Oh no you don't!' Mr Digits yelled, jumping on a hospital bed and grinning.

'Hey, Mr Digits!' Alex said.

The chimpanzee turned on Alex and snarled at him. 'I don't know how you two got back inside FallDeep, but you're going nowhere. Everyone is staying right here!'

'What?' Alex took a step back. 'What are you talking about?'

'No!' Lucy gasped, looking up at Mr Digits standing on the bed. 'Are you the one keeping us all in FallDeep?'

Mr Digits looked up at the ceiling.

'Maybe, maybe not,' he said, stuffing a finger up his nose and having a good root around.

'You're the game's avatar, aren't you?' Aurora said. 'You've become self-aware, sentient.'

Mr Digits lowered his head and stared at Aurora.

'Ooh, aren't you the clever one,' he said, and pulled his finger out of his nostril. He examined the green bogey on the end and then popped it into his mouth.

'That's disgusting,' Lucy said, screwing up her face.

'Why are you doing this?' Alex said.

Mr Digits rolled his eyes. 'Why do you think? Because I get bored, that's why. You lot, you're always leaving me here on my own. I thought it would be fun to keep you all around for a while.'

'But people are dying,' Lucy said.

Mr Digits dismissed that with a wave of his hand. 'Oh boohoo, what's a lost life here or there? They've always got another one.'

'But they don't,' Aurora said, stepping forward and peering up at the chimp. 'Not in real life, not the life outside of FallDeep. Because you've locked the game down, players are dying in real life when they die here. Haven't you noticed that no one is coming back?'

Mr Digits stuck his finger in his ear and gave it a good wiggle. 'Nope, I've been too busy having fun.'

'You've got to open up FallDeep, and let everyone out,' Aurora said.

Mr Digits pulled his finger out of his ear and examined the lump of glistening green wax on the end.

'Fancy some?' he said, pushing his finger in front of Lucy's face.

Lucy recoiled. 'No!'

'Hey, monkey boy! Are you listening to me?' Aurora shouted.

'Who are you calling monkey boy?' Mr Digits snarled, rounding on Aurora.

'You can't keep everyone here forever!'

'Yeah? Watch me!'

Aurora sighed. 'You don't understand: all these people in FallDeep? They're not like you. They have bodies outside of FallDeep that need food and exercise and time away from the virtual environment. And if you don't let them have that, they will be dead within a matter of days.'

Mr Digits stopped sucking on his finger. 'Really?'

'Yeah, really. And then you will be all on your own in here forever.'

Mr Digits pulled his finger out of his mouth and scratched his head.

'Listen to me,' Aurora said. 'If you let everyone out of FallDeep, I will stay here with you, and I will keep you company.'

Alex glanced at Lucy. This hadn't been part of the plan.

Mr Digits sat and thought for a minute and then sprang to his feet.

'It's a deal, buddy!' the chimp said, and stuck out a hand to Aurora.

She took the chimp's hand and shook it.

'Hey, I've got my exit option back,' Lucy said.

'So have I,' said Alex.

Already there was a commotion amongst the children, and some of them began popping out of existence.

'How long before everybody's out?' Lucy said.

'Across all of FallDeep?' Alex replied. 'Only a minute, I should think. Everyone will know now they can leave.'

'But we can't leave Aurora here,' Lucy said.

The chimpanzee jumped up and down on the hospital bed, screeching and jabbering.

'That was the deal, remember! That was the deal, kids!'

Alex realised that his surroundings were fading away. Somebody, Mr Digits probably, had tripped his exit option. He saw Lucy was already gone.

The next moment, Alex was sitting up in his gaming chair and pulling off his VR helmet. His heart was thumping in his chest. His mobile phone was ringing.

He picked it up and looked at the screen.

Lucy.

'Hey,' he said.

'Oh, Alex,' Lucy sobbed. 'Will we ever see Aurora again?'

Alex finally met Lucy in the real world less than two weeks after the end of the FallDeep crisis. They hugged and cried together.

After the funeral they took a walk in the spring sunshine, comfortable in their silence together.

'I never suspected, not once,' Lucy said, finally breaking the silence. 'Did you?'

Alex shook his head. 'No, I don't think anyone did.'

'But why did she keep that so secret?' Lucy said. 'Why didn't she feel she could mention it? At least to us, her friends.'

Alex looked up at the sky. 'Because in FallDeep she wasn't Aurora of this world. Here she was trapped by her wheelchair and her brittle bones and her breathing difficulties and her illnesses. In FallDeep she was strong and fast and graceful.'

'And beautiful,' Lucy said.

Alex looked at Lucy. 'She was beautiful anyway. Her avatar was an extension of her spirit, who she truly was inside her frail body.'

'Yes, and she knew she was dying, that was why we hadn't seen her for some time in FallDeep, wasn't it? But then she came back to rescue us even though she knew she probably only had days left.'

'Hours even,' Alex said. 'She kept saying that she didn't have much time, but I thought she meant us, I thought she was talking about the FallDeep situation. But she wasn't, she was talking about herself.'

'Do you think there's any possibility she might still be alive in a way, in FallDeep? That she's exploring new parts she's never seen before, living her life?'

'Maybe,' Alex said, thoughtfully.

It was an attractive thought. FallDeep's creators had claimed they had fixed the AI problem, that the environment was no longer self-aware. But FallDeep was still in lockdown, no one could get back in until an investigation had been completed and the game was certified safe once more.

Aurora had still been in FallDeep when, in the real world, her body finally gave up and died.

'If they ever open FallDeep again, would you go back?'

Alex nodded. 'Yeah. How about you?'

'I don't know,' Lucy said, thinking of all those dreadites scuttling towards her. 'Maybe.'

'We could go back together,' Alex said. 'We could look for Aurora.'

Lucy smiled. 'Before that, how about we get to know each other here, in the real world?'

Alex smiled back. 'That would be nice.'

Lucy slipped her hand into Alex's and gave it a gentle squeeze.

They turned and walked back towards the church hand in hand, in the mild spring sunshine.

• • •

'FallDeep' was commissioned by the young writers of Redhill School, Stourbridge: **Serena, Gurmeet, Alisha, Sam, Ruby, Anisa, Will, Jake, Ibraheem, Oliver, Keeli, Sonia, Katie** and **Sam.**

Learning Centre Manager: **Kate Dorrell.**

ABOUT THE AUTHOR

Brain surgeon, former Mr Universe, rock star, world champion surfer, secret agent, eloquent in twelve languages, and special adviser to the world's leaders, **Ken Preston** loves telling lies for a living.

KEN SAYS:

'At Redhill School we talked about our favourite book and film genres, fantasy, adventure and horror coming out as firm favourites. Then we generated some possible titles for our short story based around these genres, followed by looking at settings and characters. One strong idea that surfaced was of being stuck in a computer game, which became the bedrock of the story FallDeep, although other elements were included too.'

The Boy Who Held The Sun In The Palm Of His Hand

Liam Brown

I'm sitting at the back of the classroom, trying to keep my eyes open, when the door opens and Bob the Builder walks in. I don't mean a builder who happens to be called Bob. I'm talking about the guy from the stupid TV show I used to watch as a kid. The one my little brother Tahir still watches now. Yellow hard hat. Checked shirt. Blue dungarees. Tool belt slung around his waist. But it's not his choice of clothes that nearly make me topple backwards out of my chair. Rather, it's the fact he looks *exactly* like he does in the show. Head too large for his body. His eyes and mouth little more than black slashes in his skull. His features rendered in modelling clay.

And he's huge too. At least seven feet tall. So big, that he has to stoop slightly to get through the door. He is, without a doubt, the most terrifying thing I have ever seen in my life.

Weirdest of all is the way our teacher, Mr Farrell, reacts. Or rather, *doesn't* react. He just stands there in front of the SMART board and keeps talking away as if it's the most normal thing in the world for a seven-foot stop-animation children's TV character to stroll into the classroom in the middle of a lesson. I look around at my friends, and see that they too seem equally unperturbed. It's almost as if no one can see him apart from me.

I rub my eyes, wondering if I'm going crazy, but when I glance towards the door again Bob is no longer standing in the doorway. Now he's staggering across the classroom, his limbs jerky and uncoordinated as he weaves between the desks towards me. I want to scream. I want to get up and run. But my body doesn't seem to be responding. My mouth frozen. Legs like concrete. And then it's too late. He's towering over me, drill in hand. Leering at me with that awful black mouth. And he's saying something. He's saying:

'Amir? Amir! Wake up at once! I don't care how tired you are, it is totally unacceptable to sleep in the classroom.'

I blink and look up. And suddenly I see that it's not Bob the Builder standing over me. It's Mr Farrell. And he doesn't look happy.

'With us now, Amir? Good. Then you won't mind coming to my classroom at lunchtime so we can discuss strategies for staying awake during lessons.'

I nod groggily, wiping a wet patch from my chin, while the rest of the class whisper and giggle at my expense.

The rest of the morning passes painfully slowly. People laugh at me, asking if I need a pillow, or follow me around the playground at break making snoring noises behind my back. Worst of all is the fact I'm still genuinely tired. More than tired. I'm *exhausted*. I wouldn't mind, but it's not even my fault. It's not like I stayed up all night playing Fortnite or Minecraft or something. No, I was kept awake by Tahir, who insisted on crawling into my bed and kicking me for half the night. Not that it's him I'm really mad at. He was just frightened by the noises coming from downstairs. Shouting. Crying. Things breaking. It's always like that these days. Ever since Mum's boyfriend Trevor moved in. I used to lie awake at night scared myself. Now that I'm older, I tend to just ignore it. Play my music loud. Turn the TV up. Drown it out. Tahir's younger though, just six years old. He doesn't understand that it's nothing to worry about. That this just how adults behave.

Anyway, that's why I don't moan when he climbs under the duvet next to me in the middle of the night, his breath all shivery and worried, until he falls asleep. And I'm left there lying in the dark, staring at the shadows until my alarm goes off and it's time to go to school.

By the time lunch rolls around, I'm ready to collapse. All I want to do is find a quiet corner of the playground and read my book. I can't do that though, because I've got to go to Mr Farrell's room instead. When I arrive at his classroom however, there's no sign of him. There's no sign of anyone. I sigh. Typical. I'm just about to turn and leave and make the most of what's left of my lunch break, when something catches my eye at the back of the classroom.

A door.

Now this is strange, because I have lessons in this classroom twice a week, and never once have I seen a door there before. Or have I? The more I stare at it, the more I start to doubt myself. Maybe it's always been there and I've just never noticed it? After all, there doesn't appear to be anything special about it. It's just a plain door. There must be hundreds exactly like it throughout the school. All the same, something about it draws me to it. The handle almost seems to glow.

Glancing over my shoulder, I see the corridor is deserted. I know I should leave. There's still time to get to the canteen and grab something to eat if I'm quick enough. Yet, even as I tell myself I'm being stupid, I find I'm creeping across the classroom, my legs moving of their own volition. I squeeze between the desks. And then suddenly I'm there, facing the door.

When I reach out, I half expect the handle to be hot. But it's just a normal handle. Plain metal. Nothing special. Again, I tell myself this is ridiculous. That it's probably locked. That any minute Mr Farrell's going to turn up and tell me off for being here. That I really, really should get going.

Instead, I turn the handle.

The door swings back effortlessly, and I find myself peering down a steep stagger of stairs leading into darkness. The walls either side are made of crumbling brick, frosted with moss. There's a smell too. Almost like old books. Something musty and decaying. Behind me, the classroom gleams. Shiny and bright and new. The stairs, on the other hand, seem to belong to another time altogether.

Before I can talk myself out of it, I step forwards. Almost immediately, I feel a drop in temperature. It's like walking into a cave. I pull the collar of my blazer up around my neck and take another step. Then another. 'Hello?' I call into the darkness. 'Mr Farrell? Are you down here?'

There's no answer. Of course there's no answer. And now I'm no longer just scared of getting caught. I'm scared of what I might find down here. But still I keep walking, my curiosity overcoming my fear, and before I know it, I'm at the bottom.

It takes a moment for my eyes to adjust. When they do, I find I'm facing another door. This one is different, though. Carved from thick, dark wood. It looks like it belongs in a church or a castle or something, rather than a school. There's no obvious handle to it, but when I press my palm to the wood it creaks open, revealing an even darker room. The smell of decay stronger. The temperature even colder.

'Hello?' I try again as I step inside. 'Is there anybody down here?'

Underfoot, something crunches. Like grit or broken glass. My hand fumbles along the wall for a light switch, but I find nothing but smooth rock. I decide to leave. When I turn back however, I can't find the door. It's too dark to see anything, and so I feel my way along the wall, any moment expecting to touch the wooden frame of the door.

Instead, I hear a slam, followed by the unmistakable sound of a key turning in a lock. That's when I realise my mistake.

I'm stuck down here.

Locked in.

Trapped.

It's a while before I remember I've got my phone in my pocket. When I do, I'm so relieved I almost shout out loud. All I need to do is call the school office and explain where I am. They'll send someone down with a key and everything will be fine. When I get my phone out however, my heart sinks. There's no reception down here. The dull glow spilling from the screen gives me an idea though, and I switch on the torch app. The room instantly fills with a harsh white glow, revealing a large, empty space filled with rows of empty shelves. It looks like an abandoned warehouse.

I turn back towards the wall, trying to locate the door I came in through. Before I can find it however, a small voice calls out from the other side of the room, freezing me in my tracks.

'Mrs Hopkins? Is that you?'

I spin around. 'Who's there?'

'Mrs Hopkins?' the voice calls again. 'It's me, Tim. Can I go out to play now Mrs Hopkins? I promise I won't talk in class again.'

I track the light across the room until I find the speaker. A young boy, cowering behind a rack of shelves. As the light settles on him, he straightens up and walks towards me, shielding his eyes against the light.

He's around my age, with pale skin and a mop of black hair. He's wearing school uniform too but, strangely, it seems to belong to a different school. It's weirdly retro too. The collars of his shirt too long. Trouser legs flared. The fabric faded and frayed around the edges.

'Hey, Tim,' I say. 'I'm Amir. What are you doing down here? Who's Mrs Hopkins?'

'She's my arithmetic teacher. She caught me talking in class so she sent me down to the stationery cupboard.'

'Arithmetic? You mean maths?'

Tim shrugs.

'You know, I've never ever even heard of Mrs Hopkins?' I continue. 'When did you say she sent you down here?'

'It was quite a while ago. Between you and me, I'm starting to think she's forgotten all about me.'

I'm about to ask something else, when I spot another door behind him. This one has a metal plaque on it. The word 'EXIT' in green letters. 'Hey, have you tried this door?' I ask.

'No,' Tim says, hurrying after me. 'Don't do it. Trust me. You do *not* want to go in there.'

'Why not?'

'Because *she's* in there.'

'Who?'

Tim looks around, as if he's terrified someone might be listening. Then he leans in and whispers something to me.

'There's a park ranger in there?' I repeat.

'No,' Tim says, raising his voice slightly. 'The *Dark Angel* lives in there. She captured me earlier. I only just managed to get away.'

I stare at Tim, eyebrow raised. I'm waiting for him to start laughing. To admit that he's messing around. That this is all some stupid joke. He's deadly serious, though. Wringing his hands. Eyes wide with fear.

I shake my head. 'Dark Angel, huh? Cool name. Well, if it's all the same to you, I think I'll take my chances.'

Ignoring Tim's protests, I approach the door. It's made of metal, almost like a bank vault, and the handle is so stiff I have to put my phone back in my pocket for a second and use both hands to force it open. As I depress it, Tim calls out to me one last time.

'Stop! Wait!'

But it's too late. I've already opened the door, and instantly the room is flooded with light.

It takes me a second to realise I'm standing outside, in some kind of jungle or rainforest. Thick foliage fans out all around me, huge tropical leaves creating a verdant canopy overhead. There's even a stream here, crystal clear water running along a riverbed of yellow rock.

Except, something's not quite right.

When I look closer, the rock actually seems to be made of painted fibreglass. Similarly, when I squint up, I see there are artificial lights suspended from a high ceiling that's been painted to look like the sky. I find myself thinking back to Mr Farrell's classroom. How the physics of this place make no sense. I only went down a dozen steps. Yet this indoor forest seems to be housed in a space the size of a cathedral. So where on earth am I? Before I can puzzle this any further, I'm distracted by a cry.

'Hey! Hey you! Help!'

For a second, I think it's Tim again. That he's followed me through the door. But then another voice calls out. And another, and another.

'Help!'

'Over here!'

'Please!'

'Get me down!'

That's when I see them. The bamboo cages hanging from the trees. And inside each cage, a child. Scanning the trees, I see that, like Tim, they're all wearing unfamiliar school uniforms, though some look even older than his. Waistcoats. Flat caps. A couple of the girls are even wearing the same white frocks that I recognise from when we dressed up for Victorian Day a few months ago.

'Oy! Over here!' calls a voice from the nearest cage.

I look up to see a young boy in a tweed jacket and shorts.

'I say, are you going to help us down or what?'

'I-I can t-try,' I stammer, although in truth I have no idea how I'm going to get him out. The cage is suspended high over my head, so that even if I jump I won't be able to touch it. And even if I do somehow manage to get up there, the bars are thick, and bound with rope. Without a knife or something, I don't stand a chance.

'How did you get up there?' I call up to him.

The boy shrugs. 'Same way most people ended up here. I found a door and went down some stairs. See, what happened to me was, I got caught scrumping apples over the back of the playing fields. Sir sent me to the head-master's office to be caned, but on my way there I spotted a door and, well you know the rest. Next thing I knew I was hanging up here.'

I have so many questions I hardly know where to start, when something occurs to me. 'Wait, you say you were sent to be caned? When was this?'

The boy shrugs again. 'A few hours ago, I guess.'

'No, I mean, what year?'

He sighs. 'Oh, let's not start this again.'

'Start what again?'

'I've been arguing all morning with these lot about it,' he gestures to the other cages. 'Miss Crazy-Hair over there swears blind it's 1974, while that ginger boy with the weird glasses reckons it 1990-something.'

'And what year do *you* think it is?'

'Think? Why I know for a fact it's the first of June, 1923. Wrote it in my jotter just this morning. Anyway, let's stop all this blabbering. You've got to get me down before *she* gets back here again.'

'She?'

'Yeah. Woman with the scary mask. The Dark Angel, these lot call her. She's the one who's locked us up in these cages. Well her and her gang of...' He trails off, interrupted by a crashing in the bushes. 'Oh, blast! Too late. She's here. You better hide.'

I dive for cover behind a fallen log, just in time to see two axe-wielding men stomp into the clearing. They are both bare chested, with black tattoos decorating their torsos and snaking down their arms. Standing behind them is a woman, and instantly I know she's the one they've all been talking about. The Dark Angel. Tall and muscular, her face is hidden behind a steel mask that is shaped like a human skull. Strangest of all, are the enormous pair of wings sprouting from her shoulder blades, as if surgically grafted. They remind me of a swan's, only the feathers are black.

I watch as the woman takes another step forward. That's when I see him. The boy she is dragging along by the wrist behind her. A flash of pale skin framed by a mop of black hair. His old-fashioned uniform faded and frayed around the edges.

It's Tim.

As they come to a halt, the woman hurls him to the ground, where he lies cowering, his hands tucked over his head for protection. The man nearest her observes the boy for a moment before turning back to the woman. 'He's the one who escaped earlier?'

'You mean the one you *let* escape through your incompetence? Yes. I found him creeping through the forest.'

The man, who I take to be her guard, nods nervously. 'And what would you like me to do with him, my queen? Return him to his cage?'

The woman considers this for a moment, before shaking her head. 'No. He will only try and run again. I think it is time to start the ritual.'

The man frowns. 'You don't mean...?'

'Of course,' she snaps. 'Once you have finished with him, we can move on to the others. You know we only have until sun down to complete the offering.'

'Yes, your majesty.'

The man takes a step forward towards Tim, who lets out a whimper, making a pathetic attempt to scramble away.

It's then I decide to make my move. 'No!' I yell, breaking cover and diving out towards them. 'Let him go!'

The small crowd looks up in confusion as I stumble into the clearing, waving my hands. 'Don't hurt him,' I say, rather less forcefully this time.

The woman stares at me. The eyes of her skull mask seem to glow red, before she lets out a scream. 'Grab him!'

The men hurl themselves at me. Before they can reach me however, there is a dull vibration in my blazer pocket, followed by a faint bleeping sound.

The men freeze, looking suddenly terrified.

'It's just my phone,' I say, reaching into my pocket. 'Look.'

I slide out my mobile phone and hold it up. On the screen, I see I have a missed call. I realise I must finally have signal out here.

'What witchcraft is this?' the woman says, before turning back to her guards. 'What are you waiting for? Capture him!'

Neither man moves. Instead, they both stand there, staring apprehensively at my phone as if it's some kind of deadly weapon.

As they hesitate, an idea comes to me. I quickly unlock the screen and turn the torch back on, so that a small light flashes from the handset. The man nearest to me gives a small yelp of terror. 'The prophecy was true! *The boy who holds the sun in the palm of his hand*. It's him. It must be.'

In an instant, all three of them have dropped to their knees, their hands raised above their heads in surrender. 'My lord,' the queen cries out. 'I can only apologise. You are here earlier than I'd expected. We have travelled through time and space to gather the sacrifices, if it pleases you, we can complete the ritual now?'

'The ritual?' I ask, glancing at the gleaming blade of the axe. 'No! Of course I don't want you complete the ritual. That's the last thing I want.'

The three of them stare at each other in confusion. 'But my lord, the prophecy said...'

'The prophecy?' I say, thinking fast. 'The prophecy was, well, it was wrong. Or rather, er, you read it wrong. Yes that's it...'

The queen eyes me suspiciously. 'Impossible,' she mumbles.

For a moment I think I've blown it. Just then however, my phone starts to ring again, filling the air with my stupid ringtone that sounds like a robot malfunctioning. The sound makes the three adults quiver with terror.

'Please my lord!' The queen cries. 'I'm sorry! Don't punish us for my insolence. We'll do anything you say.'

'Anything? Well, you can start by sending these children back to where they came from. You *can* do that, can't you?'

'If that so pleases you, my lord?'

I nod. 'Well. That's great then. Cheers.'

The three of them stare at me, as if expecting me to say something else. I sigh, before holding up my phone up towards the sky. I flick my torch back on, before speaking in the deepest, most divine voice I can muster. 'Well what are you waiting for?' I boom. 'I *command* you to return these children to their rightful times.'

The queen scrambles to her feet, and raises her hands to the air. She chants something in a language I don't understand, almost like music, like a song, and suddenly Tim and the other children vanish.

The queen turns to me. 'Now, my lord. Will you take your seat on your throne?'

'My what?'

'Your throne, my lord. For this kingdom is yours, and we are your faithful servants.'

I look around. At the fake trees. The painted sky. The fibreglass river. Even if it's not real, it's still tempting to stay. I could do whatever I want here. No school. No teachers. No Trevor. A whole world to myself, with me as the king.

But then I think about Tahir. Scared and awake in the middle of the night, with no one to tell him everything's going to be alright.

That's when I realise I can't stay.

'I'm afraid I need you to send me back.'

The queen raises an eyebrow. 'Back?'

'From where I came from. I have to go home.'

'As you wish, my lord.'

She starts to sing again, a song as old and as sad as the Universe itself.

The world begins to spin.

And then everything goes a bright, brilliant white.

I'm standing in the corridor outside Mr Farrell's classroom. Outside I can hear the familiar roar of children playing. I'm back at school. I take my phone out of my pocket and see that it's lunchtime. I'm just about on time for my detention. I take a deep breath and walk into the classroom. There's no sign of Mr Farrell. No sign of anyone. I feel a lurch of panic as I look towards the back of the classroom. This time, though, there's no door. It's just an ordinary wall.

Before I can examine it any closer, there's a sound behind me, and Mr Farrell walks into the classroom, along with Miss Malpass. At the sight of me, they stop talking and stare in surprise.

'Amir? What are you doing here?' Mr Farrell asks. 'It's lunchtime.'

'I know, sir. You told me to come here. You gave me a detention this morning for sleeping in class?'

Mr Farrell shakes his head, confused. 'Detention? How strange, I don't remember. Maybe I was the one who was sleeping in class? Anyway, consider yourself lucky – you're off the hook.'

'You mean I can go?'

He nods. 'You're free. At least, for the next twenty-five minutes...'

I head for the door before he has time to change his mind.

As I get into the corridor however, I pause, catching sight of my reflection in one of the display boards. For the first time in as long as I can remember, there's a smile on my face, as bright and as dazzling as the sun.

• • •

'The Boy Who Held The Sun In The Palm Of His Hand' was commissioned by the young writers of Harborne Academy, Birmingham: **Hussain Alqattan, Zuhair Asif, Mohamed Bashe, William Brown, Isabelle Chan, Andrew Grube, Kodie Harding, Aliyah Hussain, Izwi Jambawo, Khyra Leary, Andreja Leliugaite, Yoonis Osman, Zahraa Qudir, Ilham Ahmed, Amir Safaryar** and **Omar Barrett.**

Teacher: **Andrew Farrell**

ABOUT THE AUTHOR

 **Liam Brown** is the author of four novels: *Real Monsters* (2015), *Wild Life* (2016), *Broadcast* (2017) and *Skin* (2019). His work has been published internationally, translated into several languages and optioned by a major Hollywood studio. He lives in Birmingham, England, with his wife and two children.

LIAM SAYS:

'Working with the group of Year 7s from Harborne Academy was a joy. From the moment I entered the classroom, I was met by an unbridled eruption of enthusiasm for all things reading-related. Indeed, when I asked the children to name their favourite novels, they each struggled to narrow their list down to twenty.

Following a wide-ranging discussion on the reasons books still matter, and what keeps people reading (despite so much electronic competition for our eyeballs, hearts and minds), we began talking about the elements they'd like to include in their story. After a heated debate, they decided it should be a thrilling mystery-comedy, featuring a dream, a dark room, a mysterious door and an ancient civilisation. They also asked me to include a 'dark angel', the children's TV character Bob the Builder, and a cameo appearance from two of their teachers. A daunting challenge!

Hopefully I've created something that they will respond to (and that lives up to their impeccable taste!). Either way, I leave the project with a renewed sense of optimism. If these young people are the future of literature, then it is in safe hands.'

3:1

Liz Hyder

The old brownstone building looms over me in the darkness as I push my way past the Keep Out signs and squeeze between the security railings. Everyone always says this is the city that never sleeps but right now, at 2am, everything feels pretty dead in this part at least. Just me, a handful of stray cats and some flickering streetlights that are definitely making me think this was a dumb idea.

I shiver to myself as I look up at the house, condemned signs and warning tape stuck all over it. What am I doing here? I don't even know Ben that well. Not really.

My phone buzzes, lighting up in my hand. It's him. *Come on up. 2ⁿᵈ floor. Mind the stairs. This is all kinds of awesome I promise! xx*

All kinds of awesome. And two kisses. He'd been raving about this place. The perfect hide-out, he'd said. Creepy, but romantic and beautiful, somewhere special. A secret just for us. His eyes had twinkled as he'd said it, his hand on mine, warm and comforting. It'd sounded like so much fun in the beautiful autumn sunshine, leaves falling from the trees around us in Central Park like confetti. But right now, in the middle of the night in pitch-blackness, all the warning signs are going off in my head. I should go home but curiosity always gets me in the end. It's what brought me here after all, why I ended up in New York in the first place. Something new, something different. A fresh start.

I take a deep breath, in and out, counting up and down to five, just like the counsellor taught me. After what happened. Before.

Slowly, I walk up the handful of stairs to the rickety front door, using my phone as a torch. I push the door open, gently at first, hearing it scrape against the dusty floor, hinges squeaking like a pig in pain. The light on my phone flickers. Damn it, the battery is lower than I thought. I swear I charged it before I left. But it's too late now. I swallow and head inside, the door creaking shut behind me, darkness all around.

The stairs are rotten. Some of them missing entirely, others flaking away. I take each step gingerly. The whole house feels like it could fall down around my ears but I keep on, slowly, steadily.

First floor. Second floor. As I go up the last few stairs I whisper 'Hello' out loud and hear it echo around me, tickling my ears and making me tense up. I step out and onto an old rug, decaying and dog-eared. I am here. But where is he?

'Hello?' I say again, louder this time but still not much more than a whisper. 'Ben?' I feel that if I speak too loudly the bricks and mortar will sigh their last and crumble away. It feels like a sacred place somehow, this abandoned house, empty and desolate.

I hold up my phone, torch shining through the dust. I'm in a large empty room, three big windows at the front of the house, curtains ragged and torn. I move my arm, shining the light around, holes in the floorboards, some big enough to fall through. I keep turning, illuminating parts of the room like a spotlight and that's when I see him.

Daniel.

My heart thunders. Breath sucked out of my lungs. The light trembles as my hand shakes.

But it can't be. It can't be, I say to myself. Impossible.

'Daniel...?' I whisper.

He's got his back turned towards me. That distinctive brown leather jacket, the one with the eagle on the back. Hair flopping to one side. But it's impossible. It can't be him.

Daniel. Daniel – that boy I loved so much it felt like we were one person. Daniel. My spring, my summer, my everything.

But Daniel is dead. I saw it myself.

The figure goes to turn and I scream. And that's when

I drop my phone, light bouncing once, twice and then disappearing through a gap in the floorboards.

Darkness.

'**O**h my word. Are you kidding me? That jacket is *grim*. It looks like something your dad would wear.'

'Shut up! No it doesn't.' Daniel joke-punches me in the arm.

'It totally does. What's the eagle for anyway? It's just weird. And brown leather, that is *not* a savoury colour, my friend.'

'It makes me look like a superhero. I had it sent over from the States. I thought you'd like it.'

'I promised you I'd always tell you the truth. You look terrible.'

'You're just saying that 'cos *you* want it. You've pretty much nicked all my clothes over the past few months.'

'That is *so* not true.'

'It so is.'

I mock-punch him back. 'I've never nicked your pants.'

He laughs. 'There's still time...' he leans in and kisses me. Warm breath, soft lips, hair flopping into my face. I pull him in closer. Run my fingers through his hair. I want this to last forever. The two of us together. Invincible. But I know it can't. America is beckoning.

'I want it to be special,' he says, murmuring into my neck as we sit on the edge of his bed. 'Our last day before you go, our last night.'

I smile as his hands wander over me. New York. Just saying it makes my heart quicken. The city that never sleeps. A new country, a new city. New opportunities. The land where anyone can become King – or Queen.

This is what true love feels like I think, as Daniel's kisses go further and further down. But I know that it's not true. This is what *desire* feels like. And who wouldn't want to give in to that? I sigh and stretch myself out.

'**Y**ou thought I was *him*, didn't you?'

A voice in the gloom. Ben. His American twang. A prank. That's all. But it can't be. My mind is racing. Daniel. He knows about him. And the jacket. It's not a coincidence. But how and –

I can't see properly. The light from my phone gone, I'm reliant on the flickering streetlights through the dirty windows. I squint to try and make things out.

'What do you want?' I say, my voice sounding so very small. 'What do you want?'

I hear footsteps slowly coming towards me. The streetlights outside flicker and die plunging us into darkness.

Think. For goodness sake THINK!

'Please!' I say. 'Please! Wait. None of it is what you think...'

The footsteps stop.

'I'll tell you what really happened – to me and Daniel,' I say. 'I promise. I'll tell you the truth.'

'All of it?' Ben asks.

'All of it,' I say. 'Every last detail.'

'The quarry? Are you serious? How is that the perfect place to spend our last day together?' I pull a face at him, looking at the handwritten invitation Daniel's just given to me.

'When did you last go up there?' he says, wonky grin on his face.

'Years ago obviously. I mean, why would I hang around up there, right?'

'You've been missing out, I tell you.'

'Have I though? *Really*?' I say, super-sarcastically.

I think back to last month. When Dad confessed that he'd taken the job in New York. Of course he had. I hadn't stopped pestering him about it for weeks on end. Mum was easy either way but come on, who wouldn't want to live in New York? Land of skyscrapers and dreams, land of movies and superstars. The city that never sleeps. I had nothing to hold me here, school had finished for the year and the summer was half gone already.

'I'll find new friends,' I'd said to Mum cheerily as we went through her wardrobe, looking for things to clear out before we moved.

'But what about Daniel?' she'd said, stopping what she was doing and fixing me with *that* look. 'I thought you were pretty serious about him.'

'Mum! You know there's this amazing invention now called a plane and they cross the Atlantic like a million times a day,' I'd said, rolling my eyes.

It's funny how your mind plays tricks. I'd convinced myself that Daniel was the love of my life – at first that is – but I knew only too well that I didn't want to grow up to be one of those people who shacked up with the first person that showed interest in them. You know the type. I wanted to live, not just a little but a lot. A lot. And New York was calling me. What would it really be like to live there? Wouldn't *you* be curious to find out? Wouldn't you do whatever it takes to try out a new life for yourself?

The quarry was deserted, had been for years. Greened mossy rocks lined the quarry walls and a deep dark pool the colour of jewels lay at the bottom, reflecting the sun back up at us.

He'd laid out a picnic, woollen rug, bottle of fizz that he'd managed to get hold of somehow, somewhere, even though we were *so* not old enough to drink. A whole spread of all my favourite things. There were empty jam jars too, candles in them that he'd light when the sun started to go.

Our last day.

Our last night.

I gulp back the tears, remembering.

'Go on,' demands Ben. 'Every last detail.' His voice shakes like he's crying too.

I didn't know what to say. I hadn't expected *this*. We were just kids right? He kneeled in front of me, hand outstretched, box open, a ring glittering at me like all the stars of the night sky.

I didn't know what to say. My parents would have gone ballistic if they'd known all we'd got up to over the past months anyway but now a ring and fizz and the sun setting over the quarry and... I was all out of words.

His face was gradually falling, elation turning to disappointment, surprise, heartbroken.

'I thought –' he slowly shut the ring back in its box. 'I don't know what I thought...'

'Daniel... please.' I reached out and he shrugged away, my fingers slipping away from him. He turned his back on me, the eagle on the back of his jacket looking as if it were glaring at me.

'What's the point?' he'd said. 'What's the point of any of this? I thought you loved me too.'

The light is bright in my eyes. Ben shines a torch directly in my face. I blink hard, trying to look away. It's like he's interrogating me.

'He loved you,' Ben says, choking back tears. 'He told me so.'

'Funny, he never mentioned you,' I say. Ben, the Ben standing in front of me isn't my on-off boyfriend of the past month, he isn't that hot guy I'd seen outside the Whole Foods store three weeks running before he plucked up the courage to talk to me. He is a stranger. Someone who knew about me and pretended he didn't. Someone who'd entrapped me. I felt my fists curl.

'Of course he didn't mention me. He was scared of what you'd think,' Ben says. 'That he'd dabbled with boys too. Swung both ways. He thought you'd drop him if you ever found out.' He snorts to himself. 'I loved him more than you will ever be capable of. That summer he went to Sweden, two years ago? That's when we met. We fell in love so hard it hurt. And then he went home. Back to England. Back to Skype and emails and photos but then he stopped calling as often. I still felt exactly as I had the first time I'd seen him but I know he didn't feel the same anymore.'

He pauses before spitting the words out. 'And then there was *you*.' I can hear him snarl. 'Did you push him?'

I gasp. 'Is that why you've dragged me up here? How can you even think that?! I would never have hurt him!'

'**H**ey, Dan, it's okay. It's fine, you can always visit,' I said casually, trying to sound reassuring as I lounged on the picnic blanket. 'It's not that far, there's technology, we can chat everyday, the time difference isn't that bad and –'

Daniel shook his head.

'It's not the same. I'm losing you, I know it.'

He turned back towards me.

'Tell me you love me,' he said, his face flushed with emotion.

I didn't say anything.

'Tell me!' he said. 'Just say it.'

'I thought I did, for a long time,' I said. 'We've had so much fun, it's been the best summer ever but –'

'But what?'

'Well, all good things must come to an end. Look, let's not spoil –'

'You never really cared for me did you?'

'Dan, of course I do. I always will. It's just –'

'Just not in the same way I do.'

He was angry. I could see that now.

'My life's not worth living if I can't have you,' he said. 'Remember that.' And then he stepped off the cliff, straight into the quarry.

I ran to the edge but he'd already gone under. He must have hit his head when he fell. I screamed, scrambling down to the edge of the quarry but I couldn't swim, I've never been able to. I rang the police, hands shaking but – well, you already know the rest.

There's silence. The light still bright in my eyes.

Was it enough? I hope so.

'You lying witch,' he says at last, voice trembling with fury. 'You little lying witch. You expect me to believe that? That ring was just a memento, he wasn't gonna propose to you. What, like some kind of teen romance, run away to Vegas, all of that? He always said you were great at making stuff up, making up stories in drama classes. I'd never have believed it if I hadn't seen it for myself. You could get an Oscar some day. He fell in at sunset right, that's what you said? So tell me this, why didn't the police get a phone call from you 'til over two hours later – huh? Two hours. What were you doing, huh?'

I stiffen. He'd read the reports. How the hell had he got hold of the reports? My name was redacted from them, wiped clean, that's what our lawyer had said.

'I can see your lies right in your eyes,' his voice is closer now. 'Your crocodile tears, fake as your hair colour.'

I sob, pretending to choke on my words.

'My boyfriend just killed himself in front of me,' I snivel. 'I wasn't thinking straight, I – '

I can feel him coming towards me, hot heat in the cool night air. I tense my body.

'Liar,' he snarls. I wait as he comes closer. Ready for him.

With every ounce of strength I possess, I throw myself towards him, pushing him as hard as I can and roaring as I do so. Hoping beyond hope that those floorboards are every bit as rotten as I think they are.

My wish is granted. He loses his balance, light from his torch throwing up to the ceiling as the wood splits, splinters, cracks and a void into the dark opens up. It welcomes him in as he plummets down one and then two floors before a perfectly ordinary sounding thud. Like a really loud version of a cat jumping off a wall. Kind of satisfying. I listen out for a groan, but there's nothing but dust and silence.

And just like that, the dodgy streetlights flicker back to life. If I believed in such things I would see it as a sign, an omen, but it's coincidence. Nothing more.

I breathe out. Count to five.

I can see my footprints in the dust behind me. My phone is who knows where? I've left too much of a trace to let things stay as they are.

I reach in my pocket and feel the smooth cool round-ness of my lighter. This wasn't what I was expecting this evening but then 'that's how the cookie crumbles', as they say here.

I reach up and smooth my hair back, touch my cheek. I am entirely unharmed. My tears dry on my cheeks. You know, I look pretty convincing when I cry. I've practised in the mirror for years. Oh I can do the whole lot, my fake laugh is so good, you'd definitely think it's real but the tears are a speciality. I can turn them off and on as easy as a faucet. That's what they call taps in America.

I gather my thoughts. Wrap them around me like a comforting blanket. Silly Ben, thinking he's cleverer than me.

I click on the lighter one, two, three times. I like the feel of the little wheel under my thumb, the smell of the lighter fluid, the glow of the flame. The red of the plastic and the yellow dragon on it.

Slowly, carefully I walk back down the stairs to the ground floor using the lighter to show me my way. A surprise awaits. My mistake. It seems Ben fell straight down to the basement. Three floors, all the way down. One. Two. Three. I look at him through the hole he made as he fell, torch illuminating his body – neck and limbs at most peculiar angles as he lies on the basement floor. What a shame, a waste of such a handsome boy. I look at his beautiful hands all bent and twisted and think how warm and soft they were over me. Like I say, a waste.

I look around and spy a rusty old bent nail on the floor. That'll do, I think and I pocket it. I like a memento.

I pick up a corner of the curtains on my way out and hold the lighter to it. It's beautiful, the fire. I watch it shoot up the curtains, hot glow lighting up the shabby rooms. I head out, wait on the other side of the street and watch as the flames take over the whole building, floor by floor. I stand there for ages, right up until I hear the first sirens in the distance before tiptoeing home.

Tomorrow morning, I will tell Mum that I lost my phone. That a weird boy had been following me, I didn't want to say anything, didn't want to worry her seeing as we hadn't been here very long.

Poor Ben. Poor Daniel too. But no, I mustn't think about it. I count to five as I breathe, lying on my back in my bed. One… two… three…

'It's just a memento!' he laughs as he hands me the ring.

'Fine, whatever,' I say, putting it on as I laugh.

'Hey and there's something else too.'

He reaches into his other pocket and his lighter falls out – the one he's always losing, bright red with a yellow dragon on it. 'Nope,' he giggles 'That's for later, for the candles – ah, here it is!'

He pulls out what looks like an envelope.

'What's that?' I say.

'A surprise…' he says, grinning. 'It's my plane ticket to come and visit you.'

My face must have fallen because he freezes.

'You wanted me to come and visit. You said so like a million times!' he says.

'Yes, sure of course but just I –'

'You didn't mean it.'

'No! I did mean it – just that I thought, look I might

need time to settle in, it's going to be weird not knowing people and –'

'But that's why I'm coming, so you've got something to look forward to, a friendly face.'

I don't know what to say to him. I thought it was obvious. It's a summer fling, right? That's it. That's all it is. Sure I mouth the words 'I love you' and all that but I don't mean it. They're just words. I thought we'd have a fun last day and then I'd be gone and then I'd be busy – or I'd say I was – and not able to Skype and he'll forget about me. Like I'll forget about him. Like I'm already forgetting about him.

'I can't believe you're doing this. I've been saving up ever since you said you were going.'

'Okay, well now I feel guilty.'

'This is just another game to you, isn't it? That's all.'

It's not though. I mean I am fond of Dan, the way he makes me feel, but I want to start again when I step off that plane. Wouldn't you, given half a chance?

I want to reinvent myself. Be the me I've always wanted to be. Here, if you change your hair or start wearing different clothes, it's a Thing and everyone won't stop going on about it for like forever. But there, no-one knows me, I can cut my hair short, dye it purple and pink and no-one will care. Have a new nickname, open new social media accounts, start again. I don't want ghosts from the past cramping my style.

So we argue. We're good at arguing. We haven't done it often enough I think, as we stand there spitting feathers at each other. He grabs my arm when I go to leave and I slap him around the face. And then he comes for me and I slip over. I'm angry now too, this is my last day with him. This was supposed to be <u>nice</u>. I pick up a rock that's near my hand and I scramble back up to standing and whack – I hit him in the face with it as hard as I can.

The blood runs down his face, a wound open on the side of his head. Woozy, he sways. His hand slowly reaches up to his face. He teeters, just for a moment on the edge. And all time stops still. What have I done?

It's only when I hear the splash that I'm jolted back into reality. I run to the edge but he's already sinking into the jewel-like water, framed like an angel, down, down into the quarry lake, darkness floating out like a cloud from his head.

It was an accident, right? Of course. Yes. It was an accident.

I look around me, the picnic, the plane tickets, the lighter. I look at the ring on my finger and I take it off, throwing it onto the ground near the discarded box.

Think. THINK.

'We had a row,' I moan, tears flowing down my face. Good. That feels real. I say it again and again, rocking myself as the sun sets.

Make it look convincing. You were born for this. Come on.

I pick up the rock, bits of blood and his hair on it and I throw it into the quarry, it sploshes as it sinks down.

I pick up his lighter and the plane ticket, shoving them into my pocket, and scramble down the sides of the quarry wall, cutting my hands as I slip, slide and fall to the edge of the lake. I look at the scratches on my hand, lines of red. Good. This will make me look desperate.

I wait at the bottom.

'Daniel!' I shout out. My voice echoes back at me. Not bad. I try again. 'DANIEL!' Better. More pleading.

I get out my phone. Patchy reception. Perfect.

I feel his lighter in my hand and click it one, two, three times before I hold out the plane ticket and set light to it. The flames crackle around the edge and, as they take full hold, I burn it until the heat singes my fingers before I drop it into the lake where it dissolves to ash. Good.

I take a deep breath, I think to myself. I think hard. I rehearse it all in my head. I go through it so many times that I even convince myself. Poor Daniel. Just a tragic accident. My grieving face is perfect.

Finally, I am ready.

I pick up my phone and dial 999.

'There's been an accident,' I weep. 'It's my boyfriend, he just – we had a row and he just –'

I breathe. In and out. Counting to five as I do so. One... two... breathing in.

I look out at the New York skyline from my bedroom window.

I just wanted a fresh start. That's all. I look at the rusty nail and the red lighter with the yellow dragon sat on my bedroom shelf. Mementos. I like a memento.

Three... Four... Five. I hold my breath for a second.

This evening is my first audition for an off-Broadway show but I already know that I'll get it. I've just got that feeling.

I twiddle the ring that Dan gave me. Round and round it goes on my finger. I put it on for luck earlier so that I didn't forget.

I breathe out. One. Two. Three...

I look at the towering buildings outside and smile to myself.

Four. Five.

• • •

'3:1' was commissioned by the young writers of Cockshut Hill School, Birmingham: **Wendy, Jordan, Bradley, Sarah, Zihad, Jannath, Kieron, Malika, Gideon, Alexandra** and **Jennifer.**

Librarian: **Karen Kaur.**

ABOUT THE AUTHOR

Liz Hyder's debut novel *Bearmouth* is published by Pushkin Press in hardback this September. Winner of the 2018 Moniack Mhor Emerging Writer Award, Liz is also an experienced creative writing workshop leader and in 2016, co-founded The Wordshoppers with poet Jean Atkin to offer a range of interactive workshops for all ages.

She is a member of NAWE (National Association of Writers in Education) and of Writing West Midlands' Room204 development scheme for writers. A past member of the National Youth Theatre, she has a BA in Drama from the University of Bristol and is on the board of *Wales Arts Review*.

The Headstrong Historian

Chimamanda Ngozi Adiche

Many years after her husband died, Nwamgba still closed her eyes from time to time to relive his nightly visits to her hut and the mornings after, when she would walk to the stream humming a song, thinking of the smoky scent of him, the firmness of his weight, those secrets she shared with herself, and feeling as if she were surrounded by light. Other memories of Obierika remained clear – his stubby fingers curled around his flute when he played in the evenings, his delight when she set down his bowls of food, his sweaty back when he returned with baskets filled with fresh clay for her pottery. From the moment she first saw him at a wrestling match, both of them staring and staring at each other, both of them too young, her waist not yet wearing the menstruation cloth, she had believed with a quiet stubbornness that her chi and his chi had destined their marriage, and so when he came to her father a few years later bringing pots of palm wine and accompanied by his relatives, she told her mother that this was the man she would marry. Her mother was aghast. Did Nwambga not know that Obierika was an only child, that his late father had been an only child whose wives had lost pregnancies and buried babies? Perhaps somebody in their family had committed the taboo of selling a girl into slavery and the earth god Ani was visiting misfortune on them. Nwamgba ignored her mother. She went into her father's *obi* and told him she would run away from any other man's house if she was not allowed to marry Obierika. Her father found her exhausting, this sharp-tongued, headstrong daughter who had once wrestled her brother to the ground. (After which her father had warned everybody not to let the news leave the compound that the girl had thrown a boy.) He, too, was concerned about the infertility in Obierika's family, but it was not a bad family: Obierika's late father had taken the *ozo* title; Obierika was already giving out his seed yams to sharecroppers. Nwamgba would not do badly if she married him. Besides, it was better that he let her go with the man she chose, to save himself years of trouble when she would keep returning home after confrontations with in-laws. And so he gave his blessing and she smiled and called him by his praise name.

To pay her bride price, Obierika came with two maternal cousins, Okafo and Okoye, who were like brothers to him. Nwamgba loathed them at first sight. She saw a grasping envy in their eyes that afternoon as they drank palm wine in her father's *obi*, and in the following years, years in which Obierika took titles and widened his compound and sold his yams to strangers from afar, she saw their envy blacken. But she tolerated them, because they mattered to Obierika, because he pretended not to notice that they didn't work but came to him for yams and chickens, because he wanted to imagine that he had brothers. It was they who urged him, after her third miscarriage, to marry another wife. Obierika told them he would give it some thought but when he and Nwamgba were alone in her hut at night, he told her that he was sure they would have a home full of children, and that he would not marry another wife until they were old, so that they would have somebody to care for them. She thought this strange of him, a prosperous man with only one wife, and she worried more than he did about their childlessness, about the songs that people sang, melodious mean-spirited words: *She has sold her womb. She has eaten his penis. He plays his flute and hands over his wealth to her.*

Once, at a moonlight gathering, the square full of women telling stories and learning new dances, a group of girls saw Nwamgba and began to sing, their aggressive breasts pointing at her. She stopped and asked whether they would mind singing a little louder so that she could hear the words and then show them who was the greater of two tortoises. They stopped singing. She enjoyed their fear, the way they backed away from her, but it was then that she decided to find a wife for Obierika herself.

Nwamgba liked going to the Oyi stream, untying her wrapper from her waist and walking down the slope to the silvery rush of water that burst out from a rock. The waters of Oyi were fresher than those of the other stream, Ogalanya, or perhaps it was simply that she felt comforted by the shrine of the Oyi goddess, tucked away in a corner; as a child she had learned that Oyi was the protector of women, the reason women were not to be sold into slavery. Her closest friend, Ayaju, was already at the stream, and as Nwamgba helped her raise her pot to her head, she asked Ayaju who might be a good second wife for Obierika.

She and Ayaju had grown up together and married men from the same clan. The difference between them, though, was that Ayaju was of slave descent; her father had been brought as a slave after a war. Ayaju did not care for her husband, Okenwa, who she said resembled and smelled like a rat, but her marriage prospects had been limited; no man from a freeborn family would have come for her hand. Ayaju's long-limbed, quickmoving body spoke of her many trading journeys; she had travelled even beyond Onicha. It was she who had first brought tales of the strange customs of the Igala and Edo traders, she who first told of the white-skinned men who arrived in Onicha with mirrors and fabrics and the biggest guns the people of those parts had ever seen. This cosmopolitanism earned her respect, and she was the only person of slave descent who talked loudly at the Women's Council, the only person who had answers for everything.

And so she promptly suggested, for Obierika's second wife, the young girl from the Okonkwo family; the girl had beautiful wide hips and was respectful, nothing like the young girls of today with their heads full of nonsense. As they walked home from the stream, Ayaju said that perhaps Nwamgba should do what other women in her situation did – take a lover and get pregnant in order to continue Obierika's lineage. Nwamgba's retort was sharp, because she did not like Ayaju's tone, which suggested that Obierika was impotent, and as if in response to her thoughts she felt a furious stab in her back and knew that she was pregnant again, but she said nothing, because she knew, too, that she would lose the baby again.

Her miscarriage happened a few weeks later, lumpy blood running down her legs. Obierika comforted her and suggested they go to the famous oracle, Kisa, as soon as she was well enough for the half day's journey. After the *dibia* had consulted the oracle, Nwamgba cringed at the thought of sacrificing a whole cow; Obierika certainly had greedy ancestors. But they did the ritual cleansings and the sacrifices, and when she suggested he go and see the Okonkwo family about their daughter, he delayed and delayed until another sharp pain spliced her back;

and months later, she was lying on a pile of freshly washed banana leaves behind her hut, straining and pushing until the baby slipped out.

They named him Anikwenwa: the earth god Ani had finally granted a child. He was dark and solidly built and had Obierika's happy curiosity. Obierika took him to pick medicinal herbs, to collect clay for Nwamgba's pottery, to twist yam vines at the farm. Obierika's cousins Okafo and Okoye visited too often. They marvelled at how well Anikwenwa played the flute, how quickly he was learning poetry and wrestling moves from his father, but Nwamgba saw the glowing malevolence that their smiles could not hide. She feared for her child and her husband, and when Obierika died – a man who had been hearty and laughing and drinking palm wine moments before he slumped – she knew that they had killed him with medicine. She clung to his corpse until a neighbor slapped her to make her let go; she lay in the cold ash for days; she tore at the patterns shaved into her hair. Obierika's death left her with an unending despair. She thought often of the woman who, after her tenth successive child died, had gone to her backyard and hanged herself on a kola tree. But she would not do it, because of Anikwenwa.

Later, she wished she had insisted that his cousins drink Obierika's *mmili ozu* before the oracle. She had witnessed this once, when a wealthy man died and his family insisted his rival drink his *mmili ozu*. Nwamgba had watched the unmarried woman take a cupped leaf full of water, touch it to the dead man's body, all the time speaking solemnly, and give the leafcup to the accused man. He drank. Everyone watched to make sure he swallowed, a grave silence in the air because they knew that if he was guilty he would die. He died days later, and his family lowered their heads in shame and Nwamgba felt strangely shaken by it all. She should have insisted on this with Obierika's cousins, but she had been blinded by grief and now Obierika was buried and it was too late.

His cousins, during the funeral, took his ivory tusk, claiming that the trappings of titles went to brothers and not to sons. It was when they emptied his barn of yams and led away the adult goats in his pen that she confronted them, shouting, and when they brushed her aside, she waited until evening and then walked around the clan singing about their wickedness, the abominations they were heaping on the land by cheating a widow, until the elders asked them to leave her alone. She complained to the Women's Council, and twenty women went at night to Okafo and Okoye's home, brandishing pestles, warning them to leave Nwamgba alone. Members of Obierika's age grade, too, told them to leave her alone. But Nwamgba knew those grasping cousins would never really stop. She dreamed of killing them. She certainly could – those weaklings who had spent their lives scrounging off Obierika instead of working – but of course she would be banished and there would be nobody to care for her son. So she took Anikwenwa on long walks, telling him that the land from that palm tree to that plantain tree was theirs, that his grandfather had passed it on to his father. She told him the same things over and over, even though he looked bored and bewildered, and she did not let him go and play at moonlight unless she was watching.

Ayaju came back from a trading journey with another story: the women in Onicha were complaining about the white men. They had welcomed the white men's trading station, but now the white men wanted to tell them how to trade, and when the elders of Agueke, a clan of Onicha, refused to place their thumbs on a paper, the white men came at night with their normal-men helpers and razed the village. There was nothing left. Nwamgba did not understand. What sort of guns did these white men have? Ayaju laughed and said their guns were nothing like the rusty thing her own husband owned. Some white men were visiting different clans, asking parents to send their children to school, and she had decided to send Azuka, the son who was laziest on the farm, because although she was respected and wealthy, she was still of slave descent, her sons still barred from taking titles. She wanted Azuka to learn the ways of these foreigners, since people ruled over others not because they were better people but because they had better guns; after all, her own father would not have been brought as a slave if his clan had been as well armed as Nwamgba's clan. As Nwamgba listened to her friend, she dreamed of killing Obierika's cousins with the white men's guns.

The day that the white men visited her clan, Nwamgba left the pot she was about to put in her oven, took Anikwenwa and her girl apprentices, and hurried to the square. She was at first disappointed by the ordinariness of the two white men; they were harmless-looking, the colour of albinos, with frail and slender limbs. Their companions were normal men, but there was something foreign about them, too, and only one spoke a strangely accented Igbo. He said that he was from Elele; the other normal men were from Sierra Leone, and the white men from France, far across the sea. They were all of the Holy Ghost Congregation; they had arrived in Onicha in 1885 and were building their school and church there. Nwamgba was first to ask a question: Had they brought their guns by any chance, the ones used to destroy the people of Agueke, and could she see one? The man said unhappily that it was the soldiers of the British government and merchants of the Royal Niger Company who destroyed villages; they, instead, brought good news. He spoke about their god, who had come to the world to die, and who had a son but no wife, and who was three but also one. Many of the people around Nwamgba laughed loudly. Some walked away, because they had imagined that the white man was full of wisdom. Others stayed and offered cool bowls of water.

Weeks later, Ayaju brought another story: the white men had set up a courthouse in Onicha where they judged disputes. They had indeed come to stay. For the first time, Nwamgba doubted her friend. Surely the people of Onicha had their own courts. The clan next to Nwamgba's, for example, held its courts only during the new yam festival, so that people's rancour grew while they awaited justice. A stupid system, Nwamgba thought, but surely everyone had one. Ayaju laughed and told Nwamgba again that people ruled others when they had better guns. Her son was already learning about these foreign ways, and perhaps Anikwenwa should, too. Nwamgba refused. It was unthinkable that her only son, her single eye, should be given to the white men, never mind how superior their guns might be.

Three events, in the following years, caused Nwamgba to change her mind. The first was that Obierika's cousins took over a large piece of land and told the elders that they were farming it for her, a woman who had emasculated their dead brother and now refused to re-marry even though suitors were coming and her breasts were still round. The elders sided with them. The second was that Ayaju told a story of two people who took a land case to the white men's court; the first man was lying but could speak the white men's language, while the second man, the rightful owner of the land, could not, and so he lost his case, was beaten and locked up and ordered to give up his land. The third was the story of the boy Iroegbunam, who had gone missing many years ago and then suddenly reappeared, a grown man, his widowed mother mute with shock at his story: a neighbour, whom his father often shouted down at age-grade meetings, had abducted him when his mother was at the market and taken him to the Aro slave dealers, who looked him over and complained that the wound on his leg would reduce his price. Then he and some others were tied together by the hands, forming a long human column, and he was hit with a stick and asked to walk faster. There was only one woman among them. She shouted herself hoarse, telling the abductors that they were heartless, that her spirit would torment them and their children, that she knew she was to be sold to the white man, and did they not know that the white man's slavery was very different, that people were treated like goats, taken on large ships a long way away and eventually eaten? Iroegbunam walked and walked and walked, his feet bloodied, his body numb, with a little water poured into his mouth from time to time, until all he could remember later was the smell of dust. Finally they stopped at a coastal clan, where a man spoke a nearly incomprehensible Igbo, but Iroegbunam made out enough to understand that another man, who was to sell the abductees to the white people on the ship, had gone up to bargain with the white people but had himself been kidnapped. There were loud arguments, scuffling; some of the abductees yanked at the ropes and Iroegbunam passed out. He awoke to find a white man rubbing his feet with oil, and at first he was terrified, certain that he was being prepared for the white man's meal. But this was a different kind of white man, a missionary who bought slaves only to free them, and he took Iroegbunam to live with him and trained him to be a Christian missionary.

Iroegbunam's story haunted Nwamgba, because this, she was sure, was the way Obierika's cousins were likely to get rid of her son. Killing him was too dangerous, the risk of misfortunes from the oracle too high, but they would be able to sell him as long as they had strong medicine to protect themselves. She was struck, too, by how Iroegbunam lapsed into the white man's language from time to time. It sounded nasal and disgusting. Nwamgba had no desire to speak such a thing herself, but she was suddenly determined that Anikwenwa would speak it well enough to go to the white men's court with Obierika's cousins and defeat them and take control of what was his. And so, shortly after Iroegbunam's return, she told Ayaju that she wanted to take her son to school.

They went first to the Anglican mission. The classroom had more girls than boys – a few curious boys wandered in with their catapaults and then wandered out. The students sat with slates on their laps while the teacher stood in front of them, holding a big cane, telling them a story about a man who transformed a bowl of water into wine. Nwamgba was impressed by the teacher's spectacles, and she thought that the man in the story must have had fairly powerful medicine to be able to transform water into wine. But when the girls were separated and a woman teacher came to teach them how to sew, Nwamgba found this silly; in her clan girls learned to make pottery and a man sewed cloth. What dissuaded her completely about the school, however, was that the instruction was done in Igbo. Nwamgba asked the first

84

teacher why. He said that of course the students were taught English – he held up the English primer – but children learned best in their own language, and the children in the white men's land were taught in their own language, too. Nwamgba turned to leave. The teacher stood in her way and told her that the Catholic missionaries were harsh and did not have the best interests of the natives at heart. Nwamgba was amused by these foreigners, who did not seem to know that one must, in front of strangers, pretend to have unity. But she had come in search of English, and so she walked past him and went to the Catholic mission.

Father Shanahan told her that Anikwenwa would have to take an English name, because it was not possible to be baptized with a heathen name. She agreed easily. His name was Anikwenwa as far as she was concerned; if they wanted to name him something she could not pronounce before teaching him their language, she did not mind at all. All that mattered was that he learn enough of the language to fight his father's cousins. Father Shanahan looked at Anikwenwa, a darkskinned, well-muscled child, and guessed that he was about twelve, although he found it difficult to estimate the ages of these people; sometimes a mere boy would look like a man, nothing like in Eastern Africa, where he had previously worked and where the natives tended to be slender, less confusingly muscular. As he poured some water on the boy's head, he said, 'Michael, I baptise you in the name of the Father and of the Son and of the Holy Spirit.'

He gave the boy a singlet and a pair of shorts, because the people of the living God did not walk around naked, and he tried to preach to the boy's mother, but she looked at him as if he were a child who did not know any better. There was something troublingly assertive about her, something he had seen in many women here; there was much potential to be harnessed if their wildness could be tamed. This Nwamgba would make a marvellous missionary among the women. He watched her leave. There was a grace in her straight back, and she, unlike others, had not spent too much time going round and round in her speech. It infuriated him, their overlong talk and circuitous proverbs, their never getting to the point, but he was determined to excel here; it was the reason he had joined the Holy Ghost Congregation, whose special vocation was the redemption of black heathens.

Nwamgba was alarmed by how indiscriminately the missionaries flogged students – for being late, for being lazy, for being slow, for being idle. And once, as Anikwenwa told her, Father Lutz had put metal cuffs around a girl's wrists to teach her a lesson about lying, all the time saying in Igbo – for Father Lutz spoke a broken brand of Igbo – that native parents pampered their children too much, that teaching the Gospel also meant teaching proper discipline. The first weekend Anikwenwa came home, Nwamgba saw angry welts on his back. She tightened her wrapper on her waist and went to the school. She told the teacher that she would gouge out the eyes of everyone at the mission if they ever did that to him again. She knew that Anikwenwa did not want to go to school, and she told him that it was only for a year or two, so that he would learn English, and although the mission people told her not to come so often, she insistently came every weekend to take him home. Anikwenwa always took off his clothes even before they left the mission compound. He disliked the shorts and shirt that made him sweat, the fabric that was itchy around his armpits. He disliked, too, being in the same class as old men and missing out on wrestling contests.

Perhaps it was because he began to notice the admiring glances his clothes brought in the clan but Anikwenwa's attitude to school slowly changed. Nwamgba first noticed this when some of the other boys with whom he swept the village square complained that he no longer did his share because he was at school, and Anikwenwa said something in English, something sharp-sounding, which shut them up and filled Nwamgba with an indulgent pride. Her pride turned to a vague worry when she noticed that the curiosity in his eyes had diminished. There was a new ponderousness in him, as if he had suddenly found himself bearing the weight of a too-heavy world. He stared at things for too long. He stopped eating her food, because, he said, it was sacrificed to idols. He told her to tie her wrapper around her chest instead of her waist, because her nakedness was sinful. She looked at him, amused by his earnestness, but worried nonetheless, and asked why he had only just begun to notice her nakedness.

When it was time for his *ima mmuo* ceremony, he said he would not participate, because it was a heathen custom for boys to be initiated into the world of spirits, a custom that Father Shanahan had said would have to stop. Nwamgba roughly yanked his ear and told him that a foreign albino could not determine when their customs would change, so until the clan itself decided that the initiation would stop, he would participate or else he would tell her whether he was her son or the white man's son. Anikwenwa reluctantly agreed, but as he was taken away with a group of boys, she noticed that he lacked their excitement. His sadness saddened her. She felt her son slipping away from her, and yet she was proud that he was learning so much, that he could become a court interpreter or a letter writer, and that with Father Lutz's help he had brought home some papers that showed that their lands belonged to him and his mother. Her proudest moment was when he went to his father's cousins Okafo and Okoye and asked for his father's ivory tusk back. And they gave it to him.

Nwamgba knew that her son now inhabited a mental space that was foreign to her. He told her that he was going to Lagos to learn how to be a teacher, and even as she screamed – How can you leave me? Who will bury me when I die? – she knew he would go. She did not see him for many years, years during which his father's cousin Okafo died. She often consulted the oracle to ask whether Anikwenwa was still alive; the *dibia* admonished her and sent her away, because of course he was alive. At last Anikwenwa returned, in the year that the clan banned all dogs after a dog killed a member of the Mmangala age grade, the age grade to which Anikwenwa would have belonged if he had not said that such things were devilish.

Nwamgba said nothing when he announced that he had been appointed catechist at the new mission. She was sharpening her *aguba* on the palm of her hand, about to shave patterns in the hair of a little girl, and she continued to do so – *flickflick-flick* – while Anikwenwa talked about winning souls in their clan. The plate of breadfruit seeds she had offered him was untouched – he no longer ate anything at all of hers – and she looked at him, this man wearing trousers, and a rosary around his neck, and wondered whether she had meddled with his destiny. Was this what his chi had ordained for him, this life in which he was like a person diligently acting a bizarre pantomime?

The day that he told her about the woman he would marry, she was not surprised. He did not do it as it was done, did not consult people to ask about the bride's family, but simply said that somebody at the mission had seen a suitable young woman from Ifite Ukpo and the suitable young woman would be taken to the Sisters of the Holy Rosary in Onicha to learn how to be a good Christian wife. Nwamgba was sick with malaria on that day, lying on her mud bed, rubbing her aching joints, and she asked Anikwenwa the young woman's name. Anikwenwa said it was Agnes. Nwamgba asked for the young woman's real name. Anikwenwa cleared his throat and said she had been called Mgbeke before she became a Christian, and Nwamgba asked whether Mgbeke would at least do the confession ceremony even if Anikwenwa would not follow the other marriage rites of their clan. He shook his head furiously and told her that the confession made by a woman before marriage, in which she, surrounded by female relatives, swore that no man had touched her since her husband had declared his interest, was sinful, because Christian wives should not have been touched *at all.*

The marriage ceremony in church was laughably strange, but Nwamgba bore it silently and told herself that she would die soon and join Obierika and be free of a world that increasingly made no sense. She was determined to dislike her son's wife, but Mgbeke was difficult to dislike; she was small-waisted and gentle, eager to please the man to whom she was married, eager to please everyone, quick to cry, apologetic about things over which she had no control. And so, instead, Nwamgba pitied her. Mgbeke often visited Nwamgba in tears, saying that Anikwenwa had refused to eat dinner because he was upset with her or that Anikwenwa had banned her from going to a friend's Anglican wedding because Anglicans did not preach the truth, and Nwamgba would silently carve designs on her pottery while Mgbeke cried, uncertain of how to handle a woman crying about things that did not deserve tears.

Mgbeke was called 'missus' by everyone, even the non-Christians, all of whom respected the catechist's wife, but on the day she went to the Oyi stream and refused to remove her clothes because she was a Christian, the women of the clan, outraged that she dared to disrespect the goddess, beat her and dumped her at the grove. The news spread quickly. Missus had been harassed. Anikwenwa threatened to lock up all the elders if his wife was treated that way again, but Father O'Donnell, on his next trek from his station in Onicha, visited the elders and apologized on Mgbeke's behalf and asked whether perhaps Christian women could be allowed to fetch water fully clothed. The elders refused – if one wanted Oyi's waters, then one had to follow Oyi's rules – but they were courteous to Father O'Donnell, who listened to them and did not behave like their own son Anikwenwa.

Nwamgba was ashamed of her son, irritated with his wife, upset by their rarefied life in which they treated non-Christians as if they had smallpox, but she held out her hope for a grandchild; she prayed and sacrificed for Mgbeke to have a boy, because it would be Obierika come back and would bring a semblance of sense back into her world. She did not know of Mgbeke's first or second miscarriage, it was only after the third that Mgbeke, sniffling and blowing her nose, told her. They had to consult the oracle, as this was a family misfortune, Nwamgba said, but Mgbeke's eyes widened with fear. Michael would be very angry if he ever heard of this oracle suggestion. Nwamgba, who still found it difficult to remember that Michael was Anikwenwa, went to the oracle herself, and afterwards thought it ludicrous how even the gods had changed and no longer asked for palm wine but for gin. Had they converted, too?

A few months later, Mgbeke visited, smiling, bringing a covered bowl of one of those concoctions that Nwamgba found inedible, and Nwamgba knew that her chi was still wide awake and that her daughter-in-law was pregnant. Anikwenwa had decreed that Mgbeke would have the baby at the mission in Onicha, but the gods had different plans and she went into early labour on a rainy afternoon; somebody ran in the drenching rain to Nwamgba's hut to call her. It was a boy. Father O'Donnell baptised him Peter, but Nwamgba called him Nnamdi, because she believed he was Obierika come back. She sang to him, and when he cried she pushed her dried-up nipple into his mouth, but try as she might, she did not feel the spirit of her magnificent husband Obierika. Mgbeke had three more miscarriages and Nwamgba went to the oracle many times until a pregnancy stayed and the second baby was born, this time at the mission in Onicha. A girl. From the moment Nwamgba held her, the baby's bright eyes delightfully focused on her, she knew that it was the spirit of Obierika that had returned; odd, to have come in a girl, but who could predict the ways of the ancestors? Father O'Donnell baptised her Grace, but Nwamgba called her Afamefuna, 'My Name Will Not Be Lost,' and was thrilled by the child's solemn interest in her poetry and her stories, the teenager's keen watchfulness as Nwamgba struggled to make pottery with newly shaky hands. But Nwamgba was not thrilled that Afamefuna was to go away to secondary school (Peter was already living with the priests in Onicha), because she feared that, at boarding school, the new ways would dissolve her granddaughter's fighting spirit and replace it either with an incurious rigidity, like Anikwenwa's, or a limp helplessness, like Mgbeke's.

The year that Afamefuna left for secondary school in Onicha, Nwamgba felt as if a lamp had been blown out on a moonless night. It was a strange year, the year that darkness suddenly descended on the land in the middle of the afternoon, and when Nwamgba felt the deep-seated ache in her joints, she knew her end was near. She lay on her bed gasping for breath, while Anikwenwa pleaded with her to be baptised and anointed so that he could hold a Christian funeral for her, as he could not participate in a heathen ceremony. Nwamgba told him that if he dared to bring anybody to rub some filthy oil on her, she would slap that person with her last strength. All she wanted was to see Afamefuna before she joined the ancestors, but Anikwenwa said that Grace was taking exams in school and could not come home. But she came. Nwamgba heard the squeaky swing of her door and there was Afamefuna, her granddaughter who had come on her own from Onicha because she had been unable to sleep for days, her restless spirit urging her home. Grace put down her schoolbag, inside of which was her textbook with a chapter called 'The Pacification of the Primitive Tribes of Southern Nigeria,' by an administrator from Worcestershire who had lived among them for seven years. It was Grace who would read about these savages, titillated by their curious and meaningless customs, not connecting them to herself until her teacher, Sister Maureen, told her she could not refer to the call-and-response her grandmother had taught her as poetry because primitive tribes did not have poetry. It was Grace who would laugh loudly until Sister Maureen took her to detention and then summoned her father, who slapped Grace in front of the teachers to show them how well he disciplined his children.

It was Grace who would nurse a deep scorn for her father for years, spending holidays working as a maid in Onicha so as to avoid the sanctimonies, the dour certainties, of her parents and brother. It was Grace who, after graduating from secondary school, would teach elementary school in Agueke, where people told stories of the destruction of their village years before by the white men's guns, stories she was not sure she believed, because they also told stories of mermaids appearing from the River Niger holding wads of crisp cash.

It was Grace who, as one of the few women at the University College in Ibadan in 1950, would change her degree from chemistry to history after she heard, while drinking tea at the home of a friend, the story of Mr. Gboyega. The eminent Mr. Gboyega, a chocolate-skinned Nigerian, educated in London, distinguished expert on the history of the British Empire, had resigned in disgust when the West African Examinations Council began talking of adding African history to the curriculum, because he was appalled that African history would even be considered a subject. Grace would ponder this story for a long time, with great sadness, and it would cause her to make a clear link between education and dignity, between the hard, obvious things that are printed in books and the soft, subtle things that lodge themselves into the soul. It was Grace who would begin to rethink her own schooling – how lustily she had sung, on Empire Day, 'God bless our Gracious King. Send him victorious, happy and glorious. Long to reign over us'; how she had puzzled over words like 'wallpaper' and 'dandelions' in her textbooks, unable to picture those things; how she had struggled with arithmetic problems that had to do with mixtures, because what was coffee and what was chicory and why did they have to be mixed? It was Grace who would begin to rethink her father's schooling and then hurry home to see him, his eyes watery with age, telling him she had not received all the letters she had ignored, saying amen when he prayed, pressing her lips against his forehead. It was Grace who, driving past Agueke on her way back, would become haunted by the image of a destroyed village and would go to London and to Paris and to Onicha, sifting through mouldy files in archives, reimagining the lives and smells of her grandmother's world, for the book she would write called *Pacifying with Bullets: A Reclaimed History of Southern Nigeria*. It was Grace who, in a conversation about the early manuscript with her fiancé, George Chikadibia – stylish graduate of Kings College, Lagos; engineer-to-be; wearer of three-piece suits; expert ballroom dancer who often said that a grammar school without Latin was like a cup of tea without sugar – knew that the marriage would not last when George told her she was misguided to write about primitive culture instead of a worthwhile topic like African Alliances in the American-Soviet Tension. They would divorce in 1972, not because of the four miscarriages Grace had suffered but because she woke up sweating one night and realised that she would strangle him to death if she had to listen to one more rapturous monologue about his Cambridge days. It was Grace who, as she received faculty prizes, as she spoke to solemn-faced people at conferences about the Ijaw and Ibibio and Igbo and Efik peoples of Southern Nigeria, as she wrote reports for international organisations about commonsense things for which she nevertheless received generous pay, would imagine her grandmother looking on and chuckling with great amusement. It was Grace who, feeling an odd rootlessness in the later years of her life, surrounded by her awards, her friends, her garden of peerless roses, would go to the courthouse in Lagos and officially change her first name from Grace to Afamefuna.

But on that day as she sat at her grandmother's bedside in the fading evening light, Grace was not contemplating her future. She simply held her grandmother's hand, the palm thickened from years of making pottery.

• • •

'The Headstrong Historian' was chosen 'because it shows the importance of education and, above all, how we make use of it.'
Giovanni, 17 years old.

Getting the Messages

Anne Fine

Like everyone else, I put off telling my parents.

Most of my close friends knew. And once Mr Heffer had soft-soled his way up behind me in the newsagent's while I was flicking through something pretty giveaway, I was fairly sure all the staff at school were in on it (and half the dinner ladies, if that rumour about Mr Heffer has any truth to it). I even reckoned Mr Faroy the grocer had guessed, and I'm not sure he even knows what we're talking about.

So that just left them, really. Mum and Dad. Sooner or later, once of life's meddlers was going to take a swing at them with the old wet sock of truth, and come out with a helpful little 'I really thought it was time you were told'.

I was a wreck from walking through our back door practically expecting to see their pale, shocked faces raised to mine. (I'm not kidding. I don't think it had even crossed their minds.) And the sheer awfulness of them not even having a clue was somehow driving me towards the dread day of reckoning. I wouldn't be at all surprised if villains have the same problem. I bet axe-murderers escape undetected from the scene of the crime, and then each knock, each phone ring, causes such a rush of stomach-clenching fear that in the end they realise one day soon they're going to walk into some police station – any police station – and give themselves up, just to be able to stretch out on their hard prison bed, and breathe in peace.

Not the best reason for confessing, perhaps. But good enough. And better than some of the others, like wanting to stop your parents making their tired old jokes about gay presenters on the telly, or simply upset them out of childish spite.

And I certainly didn't want to upset mine. I'm very fond of them, I really am. (Go on. Have a good laugh. I'll wait till you're ready.) I think they're both softies, if you want to know. And I'm the light of Mum's life. Even at my age, they're still checking on me all the time. 'All right, are you, son?' 'Good day at school, sweetheart?' That sort of thing. Not that I'm actually looking for chances to whinge about that animal Parker hurling my sandwiches into the art room clay bin, or Lucy Prescott stalking me down corridors. But, if I wanted to, I could.

But I couldn't tell them this. Each time I geared myself up, I'd get some horror-show vision in my head of how they might take it. You only need half an ear hanging off one side of your head to know how some parents react. Flora knows someone whose Mum wailed on for weeks about it all being *her* fault, then threw herself under a bus. That's something nice for Flora's friend to think about all her life. George has a neighbour whose son was banished. Banished! It sounds medieval, but it happened only last year. And I just read a novel where the father got drunk and cut the little circle of his son's face out of every single family photograph, and dropped the whole lot down the pan. The poor boy pads along to the bathroom in the middle of the night, and finds a little whirlpool of his own unflushed faces staring up at him. Chilling stuff.

And then there's Mick. We met on holiday last summer and mooched around together quite a bit. When his dad won the accumulator at the races, and Mick clapped him on the back, he made a flinch little face and moved away. I bet a heap Mick wishes he'd kept his trap shut.

So you can see why I kept putting it off. But we couldn't go on for ever. I was sick of not being able to the simplest things, like keep a proper diary, or snap at Grandpa when he makes remarks about the couple on the corner, or leave the books I'm reading lying about.

And that's how I told them. Using one of those 'special interest' books. Not quite in the way you'd imagine, but it worked. Mum and I were in Readerama a few weeks ago, and she was desperate not to let me out of sight because I was carrying most of the shopping. She didn't trust me not to put it down. Mum's view that trailing two feet behind every single shopper in town is a villain just waiting to pounce on their Priceworthy carriers, and make off down some dark alley. 'Have you got all the bags? You're supposed to have *six*,' she says to me every two minutes, and I've known her have breakdowns just from my slipping one half-empty carrier inside another without sending her warning letters in triplicate first. She drives me mad. And she has the nerve to claim she's not that keen on me, when we're in town together, doing what Gran still calls 'Getting the Messages'. But I still get dragged along, as unpaid porter, whenever Dad's not available. It's my brute strength she's after, not my advice on broccoli versus sweetcorn, or red versus green for the new lavatory brush holder, or, as on this particular morning, which cookery book to buy for Aunty Sara's birthday.

'Just take the cheapest,' I said. 'It's not as if she ever gets round to actually cooking anything out of them, after all. Just flicks through and then does chicken and chips.'

'What if she has it already?'

'Give her the receipt. Then she can bring it back and choose another. The way, *she* gets to be the one whose arms stretch down to the floor.'

Mum took the hint. 'All right,' she said reluctantly. 'You can put down the shopping. But don't move away from it. Stay where you are.'

'So what am I supposed to do?'

'Browse,' said my mother. 'That's what people do in bookshops. Have a little browse.'

I browsed. I browsed about three feet to the left (*Health Matters*). I browsed a few feet to the right (*Feminism*). I browsed forward a few feet (*Family and Society*), and back a few feet (*Cars and Mechanical*). And all the time I swear to God I never let a soul get between me and the shopping bags.

Then I got uppity. I browsed a little further away, past *Holiday Guides*, and round the back of *Stamp Collecting*. I ended up opposite *Food and Drink*, and copping a major glower from Mum, who was still choosing which of the eight million cookery books on display Aunty Sarah wouldn't change first, I doubled back through *Computers*.

Fetching up back at *Health Matters*, where I'd begun.

That's when I saw it. *Telling Your Parents: A Teenager's Guide to Coming Out in the Family*. You'd think the fairies might have put it there for me. I didn't do what you'd expect – slip it out and have a quick read while she was busy comparing *Feasts of Malaysia* with *You and Your Wok*, then creep back a few days later to read the rest. No. I simply took it off the shelf and tucked it under my arm. Then I dribbled the shopping bags one by one over to Mum at Gluttons' Corner, and stood there growing a beard down to my feet until she'd chosen.

'Right!' she said finally. 'I think I've decided. I don't think she can complain about this one.'

She waited for me to point out that Aunty Sarah can complain about anything. But I had bigger fish to fry.

I trailed her to the pay desk.

'Here,' she said, taking out her Switch card and putting *Winter Cooker: A Casserole Lover's Collection* down on the counter.

'Here,' I said, laying *Telling Your Parents: A Teenager's Guide to Coming Out in the Family* straight down on top of it.

'What's that?'

'A book.'

'What book?' she said, playing for time as if she couldn't read.

'This book,' I said to her firmly. 'This book here.'

'Take it away, Gregory!' Her voice had shot up in the stratosphere. She was positively squeaking. And the poor girl at the pay desk didn't know where to look. (Would I have done it if it had been a bloke on duty that morning? Don't ask. I'll never know.)

'I mean it, Gregory!' Her hand shot out. The book went sailing off the desk onto the floor. 'I'm not buying that for you!'

I felt so sorry for her. But still I picked it up again and put it down on top of *Winter Cookery*.

'No, Gregory! No.' She swiped it off again.

I picked it up. 'Come on, Mum.'

Snatching it from me she hurled it on the table to the side. 'No! *No!*'

102

'Yes, Mum,' I said, picking it up a third time.

'Oh, no! Oh, no! Oh, God, Gregory!' She reached for the book, but this time the salesgirl dived forward at the same time, maybe to pitch in on my side, maybe to save the book from yet another battering. When their hands met, the book slid off again onto the floor, falling open at a section called, 'Telling the Grandparents'.

'Oh, God' she wailed. 'I can't believe this is happening!' And I knew from the way it came out that the first of a thousand battles was over. Mum at least believed me.

I've never felt so dreadful in my life. I wanted to say 'I'm sorry', but I was worried she'd misunderstand, and get me wrong about the way I feel about the way I am. So I just stood there like a giant lump, watching my own mum crumple, thanks to me.

Staff training at Readerama must be brilliant. Not only can the sales force read upside down, but they know what to do at sticky moments. Glancing at the name on Mum's card, the girl said gently, 'Mrs Fisher, would you like to come through to the back and sit down for a moment? I could make you a cup of tea.'

Good thing it was my mum I'd dropped the newsflash on, and not my dad. He'd have dissolved into a puddle of tears and sat there for a week, weeping into his tea-cup. Mum's made of sterner stuff. She's kept her chin up through some moments of high embarrassment while raising me, and though this must have been about the worst, she still proved equal to the strain.

'That's very nice of you,' she said, pulling her coat straight and clutching her handbag closer. 'Most kind and thoughtful. But I'll be all right.'

The girl gave me a look, and pointed to one of those little stool things they use for getting to the upper shelves. I fetched it over. 'At least sit down,' she said to Mum. 'Just for a moment.'

'Just while you ring the books up, then,' Mum said, collapsing.

'Books', not 'book'. Did you notice? I did. So did the girl.

'It won't take a moment,' she said. But then she made a point of taking her time, sliding the card through the machine the wrong way once or twice, and rooting underneath the counter for a different sized bag, to give my mum a few moments. She even came out from behind the pay desk with the slip, and brought it over for Mum to sign. Mum's hand was shaking, but the signature looked close enough.

'There,' said the girl, managing to make it sound like 'There, there...' and making me vow I'll never in my life buy any book in any shop on the planet but Readerama.

Mum raised her head. 'Well, Gregory. We can't stay here all day. Better get home.'

And tell your dad, she might have added. But I wasn't quite so worried about that. Dad has a flaming temper, but in the end he always buys Mum's line on everything. He wasn't going to like it. Well, who would? Like anyone else, he'd like his son to grow up and marry and have a couple of kids, and not be different in any way. But not because the only thing he cares about is my being 'normal'. More because he'd be quite sure that being different – especially this way – was going to make everything in my life a whole lot more difficult. But that's not true, necessarily. And I knew that, once he was convinced this was the only way I was going to be, he'd get a grip. He wants me happy more than he wants me straight. I'm lucky there. Some people want you straight more than they want you happy.

The bus ride home was pretty quiet (if you don't count Mum saying 'Gregory, have you got all the bags?' two dozen times). Once or twice she touched my hand, as if she were about to say something. But it was not until we were walking into our own street that she come out with it.

'Let's not say anything about all this just for the moment.'

I gave her a suspicious look. What was she thinking? I wasn't old enough to know my mind? That this was something I was trying on, like some new style, or hair-cut? Did she think I was temporarily unhinged? Under someone's spell? Totally mistaken?

'Just for the moment,' she repeated. 'Just till we're sure.'

No point in climbing out of a box if you're going to climb straight back in again. 'I am sure. I've been sure for years now.'

'Well, waiting a little longer before you tell your father won't hurt, then, will it?'

'Mum,' I said. 'Give me one good reason not to tell him now.'

She looked quite hunted. 'You know how upset he's going to be, and we can't have him saying anything in front of Granny and Grandpa.'

Whoah, there! I stopped in my tracks. 'And why not?'

She stopped as well. 'Gregory, you know perfectly well why not.'

I put down the shopping, all six bags of it. 'Mum, you can't pick and choose who I keep this from,' I told her. 'It's too important. That has to be *my* decision.'

'But what if your grandpa finds out?'

'It's not a matter of him 'Finding out',' I said. 'Somebody has to tell him. Otherwise I'll be back exactly where I was before, having to watch myself all the time.'

'Is that so terrible?'

'Yes, it is!' I snapped. 'And it won't stop there, either. Within a week or so, you and Dad will be trying to kid yourselves it was all just a horrible mistake. No, I'm sorry, Mum. I'm not going back and it isn't fair to ask me.'

'Fair?' she missed, striding off down the street again. '*Fair*? And what about what's fair on the rest of us? You'll give your grandpa a heart attack!'

I'd got her there. 'Oh, I don't think so,' I said, picking up everything and trailing after her. 'Didn't he go ballistic when you told him that Ginny was pregnant by Wayne Foster? And Gran cried for *weeks*. They were so upset and furious, they didn't even go to the wedding. And now look at them! Gran spends her whole life tangled up in pink knitting wool, and Grandpa won't put the baby down. They're tough. They'll get over it.'

Mum strode on furiously. 'Don't kid yourself they're going to come to terms with this quite so easily!'

'I don't see why not,' I said sullenly. 'They've got used to my terrible hair. And my terrible clothes. And my terrible music. And my terrible friends. And my –'

'Gregory! This is a whole lot more important than any of those!'

'Yes!' I yelled back. 'It certainly is! And that's exactly why I can't go on pretending all the time – not at school, and on the team, and with girls, and at home, and at my Saturday jobs, and *everywhere*. There's got to be *somewhere* I can just be *me*.'

Perhaps I'd got through to her. Or perhaps it was because we'd practically reached our own gate. But suddenly, she seemed to soften a little. 'But surely waiting a little is only sensible. What if you change your mind?'

If this had been school debate, I'd have come back at her pretty sharpish on that one, saying something like, 'I don't recall you ever saying that you'd put off marrying Dad in case you found out later that you were lesbian.' But this is my mum, don't forget. If I'd said that, she would have slapped me so hard, I'd have gone reeling into Mr Skelley's hedge. So I said nothing.

She peered in my face. 'Oh, Gregory. This is going to take a whole lot of getting used to, and I can tell you one thing. The worst isn't over.'

'It is for me,' I told her quite truthfully.

And what if I did mean the lying, the secrets, the worrying, the pretending? Give me a break! She thought I meant

107

that telling her had been the hardest thing. And that was important to her, you could tell. Shocked and upset as she was, you could still see she took it as a compliment that she mattered most, accepting it seriously, the same way she accepted my blotchy finger paintings from nursery, and my cracked pottery jewellery pot from primary school, and my split, wobbly stock cube dispenser from secondary school woodwork. Her mouth even twitched a little, as if, if she didn't have to go in there and help me through Round Two with Dad, she might even have given me the tiniest of smiles.

I pushed the gate open. 'Ready?' I said, the same way she always used to say it to me when I was starting at a new school or a new club.

'I suppose so,' she muttered, exactly the same way I must have said it to her so many times before.

On our way up the path, she suddenly stopped and hurled herself into one of my shopping bags. Scattering socks and lightbulbs, she dragged out *Telling Your Parents: a Teenager's Guide*, and hurried off around the side of the house.

I set off in pursuit. 'What are you doing?'

'Stuffing this in the dustbin.'

'What, my *book*?'

But it was already gone, deep under the tea leaves and old carrot peelings.

'It's not *your* book,' she said, slamming the lid down over the horrid mess. 'It's my book. I'm the one who paid for it.' She brushed tea leaves off her hands and added bitterly, 'Though I can't think why. You seem to be managing perfectly well without it.'

'But why shove it in the dustbin?'

'Listen, young man,' she warned me dangerously. 'Don't push your luck. If you're planning on making me *live* by the bloody book, I'll be damned if I *dust* it.'

I know when a job's done. I just picked up the messages and followed her in to face more of the music.

• • •

'Getting the Messages' was chosen by the reading group Mare di Libri in Rimini because 'it deals with the topic of homosexuality in an ironic and fun way.'

The kids chose it because it tells the story of a homosexual boy and in their opinion these stories are not usually told.

The Lady in the Looking-Glass: A Reflection

Virginia Woolf

People should not leave looking-glasses hanging in their rooms any more than they should leave open cheque books or letters confessing some hideous crime. One could not help looking, that summer afternoon, in the long glass that hung outside in the hall. Chance had so arranged it. From the depths of the sofa in the drawing-room one could see reflected in the Italian glass not only the marble-topped table opposite, but a stretch of the garden beyond. One could see a long grass path leading between banks of tall flowers until, slicing off an angle, the gold rim cut it off.

The house was empty, and one felt, since one was the only person in the drawing-room, like one of those naturalists who, covered with grass and leaves, lie watching the shyest animals – badgers, otters, kingfishers – moving about freely, themselves unseen. The room that afternoon was full of such shy creatures, lights and shadows, curtains blowing, petals falling – things that never happen, so it seems, if someone is looking. The quiet old country room with its rugs and stone chimney pieces, its sunken book-cases and red and gold lacquer cabinets, was full of such nocturnal creatures. They came pirouetting across the floor, stepping delicately with high-lifted feet and spread tails and pecking allusive beaks as if they had been cranes or flocks of elegant flamingoes whose pink was faded, or peacocks whose trains were veined with silver. And there were obscure flushes and darkenings too, as if a cuttlefish had suddenly suffused the air with purple; and the room had its passions and rages and envies and sorrows coming over it and touting it, like a human being. Nothing stayed the same for two seconds together.

But, outside, the looking-glass reflected the hall table, the sun-flowers, the garden path so accurately and so fixedly that they seemed held there in their reality unescapably. It was a strange contrast – all changing here, all stillness there. One could not help looking from one to the other. Meanwhile, since all the doors and windows were open in the heat, there was a perpetual sighing and ceasing sound, the voice of the transient and the perishing, it seemed, coming and going like human breath, while in the looking-glass things had ceased to breathe and lay still in the trance of immortality.

Half an hour ago the mistress of the house, Isabella Tyson, had gone down the grass path in her thin summer dress, carrying a basket, and had vanished, sliced off by the gilt rim of the looking-glass. She had gone presumably into the lower garden to pick flowers; or as it seemed more natural to suppose, to pick something light and fantastic and leafy and trailing, traveller's joy, or one of those elegant sprays of convolvulus that twine round ugly walls and burst here and there into white and violet blossoms. She suggested the fantastic and the tremulous convolvulus rather than the upright aster, the starched zinnia, or her own burning roses alight like lamps on the straight posts of their rose trees. The comparison showed how very little, after all these years, one knew about her; for it is impossible that any woman of flesh and blood of fifty-five or sixty should be really a wreath or a tendril. Such comparisons are worse than idle and superficial – they are cruel even, for they come like the convolvulus itself trembling between one's eyes and the truth. There must be truth; there must be a wall. Yet it was strange that after knowing her all these years one could not say what the truth about Isabella was; one still made up phrases like this about convolvulus and traveller's joy. As for facts, it was a fact that she was a spinster; that she was rich; that she had bought this house and collected with her own hands – often in the most obscure corners of the world and at great risk from poisonous stings and Oriental diseases – the rugs, the chairs, the cabinets which now lived their nocturnal life before one's eyes.

Sometimes it seemed as if they knew more about her than we, who sat on them, wrote at them, and trod on them so carefully, were allowed to know. In each of these cabinets were many little drawers, and each almost certainly held letters, tied with bows of ribbon, sprinkled with sticks of lavender or rose leaves. For it was another fact – if facts were what one wanted – that Isabella had known many people, had had many friends; and thus if one had the audacity to open a drawer and read her letters, one would find the traces of many agitations, of appointments to meet, of up braidings for not having met, long letters of intimacy and affection, violent letters of jealousy and reproach, terrible final words of parting – for all those interviews and assignations had led to nothing – that is, she had never married, and yet, judging from the mask-like indifference of her face, she had gone through twenty times more of passion and experience than those whose loves are trumpeted forth for all the world to hear. Under the stress of thinking about Isabella, her room became more shadowy and symbolic; the corners seemed darker, the legs of chairs and tables more spindly and hieroglyphic.

Suddenly these reflections were ended violently and yet without a sound. A large black form loomed into the looking-glass; blotted out everything, strewed the table with a packet of marble tablets veined with pink and grey, and was gone. But the picture was entirely altered. For the moment it was unrecognisable and irrational and entirely out of focus. One could not relate these tablets

113

to any human purpose. And then by degrees some logical process set to work on them and began ordering and arranging them and bringing them into the fold of common experience. One realised at last that they were merely letters. The man had brought the post.

There they lay on the marble-topped table, all dripping with light and colour at first and crude and unabsorbed. And then it was strange to see how they were drawn in and arranged and composed and made part of the picture and granted that stillness and immortality which the looking-glass conferred. They lay there invested with a new reality and significance and with a greater heaviness, too, as if it would have needed a chisel to dislodge them from the table. And, whether it was fancy or not, they seemed to have become not merely a handful of casual letters but to be tablets graven with eternal truth – if one could read them, one would know everything there was to be known about Isabella, yes, and about life, too. The pages inside those marble-looking envelopes must be cut deep and scored thick with meaning. Isabella would come in, and take them, one by one, very slowly, and open them, and read them carefully word by word, and then with a profound sigh of comprehension, as if she had seen to the bottom of everything, she would tear the envelopes to little bits and tie the letters together and lock the cabinet drawer in her determination to conceal what she did not wish to be known.

The thought served as a challenge. Isabella did not wish to be known – but she should no longer escape. It was absurd, it was monstrous. If she concealed so much and knew so much one must prize her open with the first tool that came to hand – the imagination. One must fix one's mind upon her at that very moment. One must fasten her down there. One must refuse to be put off any longer with sayings and doings such as the moment brought forth – with dinners and visits and polite conversations. One must put oneself in her shoes. If one took the phrase literally, it was easy to see the shoes in which she stood, down in the lower garden, at this moment. They were very narrow and long and fashionable – they were made of the softest and most flexible leather. Like everything she wore, they were exquisite. And she would be standing under the high hedge in the lower part of the garden, raising the scissors that were tied to her waist to cut some dead flower, some overgrown branch. The sun would beat down on her face, into her eyes; but no, at the critical moment a veil of cloud covered the sun, making the expression of her eyes doubtful – was it mocking or tender, brilliant or dull? One could only see the indeterminate outline of her rather faded, fine face looking at the sky. She was thinking, perhaps, that she must order a new net for the strawberries; that she must send flowers to Johnson's widow; that it was time she drove over to see the Hippesleys in their new house. Those were the things she talked about at dinner certainly. But one was tired of the things that she talked about at dinner. It was her profounder state of being that one wanted to catch and turn to words, the state that is to the mind what breathing is to the body, what one calls happiness or unhappiness. At the mention of those words it became obvious, surely, that she must be happy. She was rich; she was distinguished; she had many friends; she travel led – she bought rugs in Turkey and blue pots in Persia. Avenues of pleasure radiated this way and that from where she stood with her scissors raised to cut the trembling branches while the lacy clouds veiled her face.

Here with a quick movement of her scissors she snipped the spray of traveller's joy and it fell to the ground. As it fell, surely some light came in too, surely one could penetrate a little farther into her being. Her mind then was filled with tenderness and regret... To cut an overgrown branch saddened her because it had once lived, and life was dear to her. Yes, and at the same time the fall of the branch would suggest to her how she must die herself and all the futility and evanescence of things. And then again quickly catching this thought up, with her instant good sense, she thought life had treated her well; even if fall she must, it was to lie on the earth and moulder sweetly into the roots of violets. So she stood thinking. Without making any thought precise – for she was one of those reticent people whose minds hold their thoughts enmeshed in clouds of silence – she was filled with thoughts. Her mind was like her room, in which lights advanced and retreated, came pirouetting and stepping delicately, spread their tails, pecked their way; and then her whole being was suffused, like the room again, with a cloud of some profound knowledge, some unspoken regret, and then she was full of locked drawers, stuffed with letters, like her cabinets. To talk of 'prizing her open' as if she were an oyster, to use any but the finest and subtlest and most pliable tools upon her was impious and absurd. One must imagine – here was she in the looking-glass. It made one start.

She was so far off at first that one could not see her clearly. She came lingering and pausing, here straightening a rose, there lifting a pink to smell it, but she never stopped; and all the time she became larger and larger in the looking-glass, more and more completely the person into whose mind one had been trying to penetrate. One verified her by degrees – fitted the qualities one had discovered into this visible body. There were her grey-green dress, and her long shoes, her basket, and something sparkling at her throat. She came so gradually that she did not seem to derange the pattern in the glass, but only to bring in some new element which gently moved and altered the other objects as if asking them, courteously, to make room for her. And the letters and the table and the grass walk and the sunflowers which had been waiting in the looking-glass separated and opened out so that she might be received among them. At last there she was, in the hall. She stopped dead. She stood by the table. She stood perfectly still. At once the looking-glass began to pour over her a light that seemed to fix her; that seemed like some acid to bite off the unessential and superficial and to leave only the truth. It was an enthralling spectacle. Everything dropped from her – clouds, dress, basket, diamond – all that one had called the creeper and convolvulus. Here was the hard wall beneath. Here was the woman herself. She stood naked in that pitiless light. And there was nothing. Isabella was perfectly empty. She had no thoughts. She had no friends. She cared for nobody. As for her letters, they were all bills. Look, as she stood there, old and angular, veined and lined, with her high nose and her wrinkled neck, she did not even trouble to open them.

People should not leave looking-glasses hanging in their rooms.

• • •

'The Lady in the Looking-Glass: A Reflection' was chosen because 'Virginia Woolf managed to perfectly define the concept of the double. The lady, the story's protagonist, is describe either as a beautiful and elegant woman or as aged and unhappy. It depends on how we look at things, like in a mirror.'

This philosophy of the double, going beyond the mirror and appearances was very appreciated.

Escape

Anders Totland

Translated from Norwegian by Nancy Langfeldt

We smiled hopefully at each other, before the storm. Dizzy butterflies whirled in my stomach. I found it impossible to tell if it felt good or bad. I knew I should be happy. At least in one sense. I knew exactly how urgently we needed to get away. And what could happen if we stayed behind. I had to get away, and the whole family had helped me make it. It was no small feat.

I should absolutely have been happy. But still there was something holding me back. Something that dimmed the joy, in a way I couldn't put into words.

You nodded carefully from the other side of the flatbed, and drew your coat up over your face as the wind picked up. Could it be you felt the same way?

119

More of us had wanted to leave. Mio fought hard for the opportunity to try. He believed his chances were better than mine. Besides, he was older and ought to have been first in line to get away.

But Uncle said no.

It had to be me.

End of conversation.

Mio's expression was unmistakeable. He knew. But he didn't say anything. He didn't want to challenge Uncle, who had fixed his eyes on him as soon as he piped up. It was clear that they had already discussed it.

Explaining it all to Alina was the worst bit.

'Why can't we all just go together?' she said, looking at Uncle wide-eyed.

I felt the lump in my throat grow as Uncle explained it. Why it was just me leaving. Me and you. It's about money, Uncle said. And, as far as it goes, that was true. It was money that meant more of us couldn't leave. It wasn't just a matter of getting on the bus and catching a flight. Getting away came at a price. Money we didn't have. Our families had just about scraped together enough to cover the two of us. Sending more people wasn't an option.

'If we can't all go together, I don't want him to leave at all,' Alina said when Uncle had explained it over and over.

She was angry now, she hit him in the chest with her clenched fist, repeating the same words. Not fair, not fair, not fair.

'Don't go,' she begged.

Her tears stung like acid. Her words were barbed wire that I couldn't avoid as I stood up to leave.

I couldn't bear to look her in the eyes.

Couldn't explain to my little sister why I had to go.

Couldn't say that we would see each other again.

I didn't want to lie.

So I left.

We'd only made it a mile from town when the blizzard enveloped us. It happened faster than usual. From one second to the next the air transformed into a freezing inferno. We had to press ourselves into the sideboards of the flatbed, at the same time using our arms to cover our faces.

As long as we didn't have to stop. Not this close to town.

I peered at the people around me. Apart from you, I recognised just two others. A boy from the neighbourhood and his little sister. I didn't know them well. I just knew who they were. All the others were unfamiliar.

I breathed out, relieved. As long as I didn't know them, chances were they wouldn't know who I was either. Who I had been.

Uncle had been on his way home from the shop when two skinheads pulled him to one side.

'We know what they are,' the older of the two said, with his index finger trembling in the air.

At first Uncle didn't understand a thing. Almost nothing. At least he thought it best to look unknowingly at the threatening men.

The younger one took over. 'Don't you understand they bring shame to your whole family, to the whole neighbourhood. They need to get gone!'

Uncle was no longer in any doubt. Of course he had had his suspicions, but he'd never dared to quite think it through. Anything can be explained away if the alternative is painful enough. He had strangled the thoughts before they could develop into speculation and suspicion. It had been for the best, Uncle reasoned.

But the thought was no longer a thought; it was a full grown suspicion and not just in Uncle's mind. The skinheads had picked up the trail.

In the worst case...

Uncle didn't want to risk even thinking it.

I knew very well what I was putting at risk. As did you. I'm sure of it. Even if we preferred not to believe them, we'd heard the stories about men who'd been jailed and tortured, without a shred of proof. And they were the lucky ones. Others had simply disappeared like dewdrops in the sunshine. A suspicion raised in the right quarters was more than enough.

We knew the risks, but we couldn't resist. We'd tried for too long to keep our feelings buried, but it didn't work. Not in the long run. Not without losing ourselves, and it wasn't worth it.

We knew it now.

Who we were.

What we were.

It was so unjust I couldn't put words to it. What was a suspicion exactly?

And besides so what if they could prove it? What kind of criminal activity were we actually guilty of? In my wildest dreams I couldn't understand what I had done wrong. What I was doing wrong. How could it be a mistake, when it felt so right? It just didn't fit together.

Even so I knew exactly what the consequences could be, if I was discovered. What had to happen, sooner or later.

Of course – it hadn't been straight forward even before the uprising. But as long as you didn't parade around the streets, things were generally okay.

Now everything was turned on its head and the skinheads had eyes and ears everywhere.

There were many of us leaving at the same time. Young and old, and parents carrying children in their arms.

We had to walk for long periods. We had just got started on the day's route, when you noticed one of the fathers was struggling to keep up.

'It's my foot,' said the man. 'I think it's infected.'

I heard what he said, but didn't understand what was happening. Surely there was far too much at stake here to stop and discuss sore feet?

'Here,' you said, stretching out your arms and taking the child, as if it was the most natural thing in the world. Two others supported the father so he could stay with us.

You had developed a hacking cough after we left home, and were on the point of breakdown when we reached the next switch over and were stowed on a new lorry. The stranger with the injured foot had his son back on his lap and the boy was sleeping heavily, resting on his father's chest. I could see his foot trembling slightly, even though he tried to sit still.

You lay against me, listless. You were soaked with sweat and coughed until you gagged. It was clear that you had pushed your body to extremes. And we were hardly halfway.

'Why did you do it?' I whispered so the others wouldn't hear me. I thought about what Uncle had told me before we left: 'Just remember your goal.' I knew the elders had discussed it and that your father had said the same. The only thing we were supposed to think about was getting there safely. It was all for nothing if we didn't make it.

I looked right at you as you answered: 'Why didn't you do it?'

I couldn't stop thinking about what you had said. 'Why didn't you do it?' I didn't have an answer. I couldn't think of anything to say. I just thought about what Uncle had said. Our orders were very clear – to think only of ourselves. We were to steer clear of anything that might lead to trouble.

Under no circumstances were we to single ourselves out to the smugglers or our fellow travellers. The best way to survive was to be invisible. That's what Uncle had said. 'If no one notices you, we can at least hope that everything will end well.'

The look on his face had left little doubt about his feelings. The words he used too. He almost spat them out.

'If you had considered the consequences, and just been normal, we wouldn't be here,' Uncle had said. 'Your brother would be going as we'd planned. That's who we had saved the money for. Not for you. But now... I have no choice. We have no choice.'

That's not what he'd thought at first. When the skinheads contacted him again, he understood what they were really after. Even the worst secrets can be hidden, if you can afford it. But Uncle refused. He said they couldn't prove anything. That it was all a lie. And he knew that paying up would still be interpreted as a confession.

The next time they came back, Uncle stood in the doorway, stretching to his full height. He knew he had the whole clan behind him, people who held important positions. As long as he didn't have to explain exactly what the conflict was about, he knew he could take them on. Even these brutish fanatics had to understand they couldn't charge about town with no consequences.

The younger one had fished a phone out of his pocket. He said nothing. He just rapidly swiped his way to a YouTube video, pressed play and held it up towards Uncle.

Uncle didn't recognise any of the shackled men in the video. But he saw what happened to them, before he closed his eyes and felt his dinner rise up from his stomach.

I couldn't get it to fit together. What were you thinking? You had to understand that people noticed you. That you stood out. You had to understand that.

Fair enough, there were others who did the same. You weren't the only one. But just that was at least as good a reason to let it go. You didn't have to be the one at the forefront. More eyes on us was the last thing we needed.

But you didn't care. You didn't give a toss about what the elders had said. You completely ignored the danger you put yourself in.

And what about me? Surely everyone else realised that we were travelling together, that we had some sort of bond?

I wanted to take you to one side and talk you out of it but didn't have the guts. Each time I tried to build up to it, I thought about what you'd said. Those unjust words which even so managed tighten their grip on my stomach: 'Why didn't you do it?'

We crossed the ocean in the middle of the night. I shivered, even though it wasn't cold. I was terrified of open water, but I knew this was our only chance.

The youngest and the eldest were packed in the middle of the boat. We had to sit around the outside, with the rest of the young men. We held onto each other and hoped we wouldn't need the thin life-vests we had been given.

We had paid a handsomely for the crossing and the equipment but I had no illusions. Long before we left home I had read online about boat crews filling the vests with newspaper.

On the beach there were whispers about a boat which had capsized the day before. Sixty-five people had drowned. Almost thirty of them were children.

If the boat went down, all hope was lost. All we could do was sit still, while the waves whipped up our stomachs.

When we at last landed, we found the little girl from our neighbourhood, dissolving in tears. She had shouted until her voice broke. No amount of searching could find her brother.

We helped her look, but didn't find him. When we had to carry on, he was still lost.

The girl refused to continue without her brother. She had to find him first, she said. But you put your arm around her and drew her with you.

'I can't survive without him,' she cried and tried to push you away. But you wouldn't let her go. You just held her tighter and let her tears soak your jumper.

'There, there,' you said. 'Everything will be okay. No one is going to hurt you. I will look after you.'

'**D**o you never get scared?' I asked, as we lay under the open sky and looked up at the stars, after the others had fallen asleep.

I couldn't remember seeing them so clearly ever before. There was always light interrupting their shine. Out here in no man's land it was completely different. Without human inhabitants nature had free reign.

'Of course I get scared,' you replied. 'Everyone does.'

'But...' I searched for the right words. 'You do dangerous things. People notice you. You must understand that's not a good thing. Don't you remember what Uncle said? And your father. I know he said the same thing to you.'

You shook your head.

'Of course I remember,' you said. 'But they're wrong. I don't accept that the only thing which matters is surviving. That the worst you can do is be noticed. What you do with the time you're given – that's what really means something. And neither fathers nor uncles can control that.'

I felt the distance between us grow where we lay. And not just because you turned around and inched away, stabbing me with your last words and twisting the knife. 'I would have expected you, of all people, to understand.'

There were only supposed to be a couple of days left until we would reach the last but one border. From there we would travel on by plane and in just one more day, we would arrive at our destination.

Most of the group were long gone. Some had become exhausted, others had already reached their goal. There were just a handful of us left.

I felt the excitement build in my body. The new country was within reach. We were going to make it. We'd made it. Thousands of kilometres from home I felt safe at last.

We had to cover the last stretch on foot. We were just a few hundred metres from the border when we were confronted by two police cars. Four people emerged from the cars and started gesticulating.

We were told to sit in the ditch, while the uniformed men went through our belongings. There wasn't much to search. Most of the little we'd brought with us had disappeared shortly after we left. The rest we had to leave on the beach before we boarded the dinghy.

The radio in one of the police cars crackled, and suddenly everyone was busy. The one that looked like he was in charge pointed at another who stayed behind while the rest of them hurried away in one of the cars.

At first he seemed uneasy. He walked back and forth and looked at his watch, as if he was waiting for something. But no one came, and nothing happened.

In the end he came to rest by the little girl, our neighbour. He just stood there and looked at her. For a long time. Let his gaze wander up and down, with hungry eyes, before he motioned for her to get in the car.

A thousand thoughts flew through my mind when I saw you get up to follow the girl and the policeman. There was no doubting what the policeman had in mind. I felt my heart tighten in my chest. Still, thinking about what would happen if you tried to stop him was far worse.

We had barely spoken in the last few days. I had tried several times, but couldn't manage it. I didn't know where to start. What to say.

Obviously you were right. I had understood that. Straight after you said it, I had realised how absurd it was to let Uncle dictate how I should live my life, to hand control over to the elders and their Stone Age prejudices. If I had done that to start with, I would never have met you. Not like that, at least. And anything else was totally unthinkable. A life alone was no life at all. I knew that now.

Acting on impulse I grabbed your arm and pulled you back down, leaving you sprawling in the ditch.

'What are you doing?' You strangled your shout to a whisper, your throat pulsating.

'Don't you understand?' I said.

I wanted to shout that I was saving us both, that I couldn't live without you. The others could say what they wanted, we were nearly there, ready for our new life. At last we could be together, without hiding. At last it was going to be the two of us, properly.

But the words wouldn't come and besides, you weren't listening. You didn't want to listen. You blocked out the sound of my voice, begging you to stop, to sit back down.

And then the other car, which was on its way back, full throttle.

Four wheels throwing up sand as the brakes dug in.

Three pairs of boots hammering along the asphalt.

Two rapid shots through the open back door.

One lifeless body on the ground.

ABOUT THE AUTHOR

Anders Totland (born 1986) is an author, organist, cook and journalist. He debuted in 2015 with *The Vampires in the Apple Garden* and has distinguished himself as one of Norway's most exciting young adult writers in recent years. In 2016 he received the Nynorsk Children's Literature Prize for his first novel, *Angel in the Snow*.

Forever Yours

Agnes Matre

Translated from Norwegian by Nancy Langfeldt

The thermometer has hit twenty-eight degrees, unusual for Vestlandet. I want rain, thunder, yes a terrible storm. I want to abolish gravity, tear down natural law, but today not even the sky will listen to me. Instead it hungrily clutches the sunshine and cuts through the steel reinforcements of control which have been keeping me from collapsing. Which have kept me upright since I, one Saturday morning six months ago, found out what was coming.

If the heavens were paying attention, they would let the rain pour. Let me drown in it, rather than witness this. I look at the clock. Soon the church bells will ring for him, and I have decided to be there when they do.

I found out from a friend of a friend of his. It was the first time I understood that I no longer had anything to do with him. I lean out of the upstairs window. My bedroom still has Beyoncé posters on the walls. I didn't take them down when I moved in with him, and I didn't have the will to do it when I moved back here, one year later.

In the shower I lather the soap all over my body. Inch by inch I let my hands move tentatively, as if to check if I remember how he used to slowly caress my hips. My hands move almost autonomously, my fingers are his fingers. I close my eyes, grip his hair, bend his head back and pull him towards me, kiss him hard, almost desperately, until I let my lips soften against his. I feel the rough stubble scrape my cheek, my breasts and stomach, while I'm showered with water and love. Then I feel him against me down there. A memory.

My legs tremble as I grip my towel. I dry myself. My back will have to dry on its own. Then I smooth lotion over my body, rub it firmly into my skin, let it lie there as a barrier against what I'm about to go through. I do up the wristwatch he gave me, check the time and hesitate for a couple of seconds before I find my engagement ring in my jewellery box. *Forever yours.* The ring slides onto my finger and settles in place like it's always been there.

I fetch my dress from the wardrobe. 'I love it and I love you,' I can hear him say. He is in my stomach, in the room and smooths his hands over the white skirt. 'It ought to be your wedding-dress,' he says enthusiastically, just behind me, like he used to be, his breath on my neck.

I pull the dress over my head, meet the white fabric in the mirror as the sun drags itself in through the window and dazzles me. My hands are shaking as I pull on my tights. My shoes are new. Everything is new. Everything is pristine. I thread the ring onto my ring finger. I can see him in the church, with her. I can see her ring, his ring. I wonder where they're hiding them. I hang the dress back in the wardrobe. Instead I put on a dark pair of trousers and a suit jacket, then check everything is in my handbag before I leave.

At the church I stand in the shade under a copper beech tree, to one side of the main entrance. I don't need telling that I don't belong here, but several people feel the need to silently let me know when they see me. Some smile sympathetically. It's intolerable. I don't want to be here, but I have to be. Just to see for myself how things are now.

The fabric of my trousers is scratchy against my thigh, the jacket is too tight, it's rubbing under the arms, the buttons of my blouse are cold against my body from waiting in the shade while everyone else went inside. I sit down in the back row and listen to conversations between people I once knew. Just before the ceremony begins, his grandmother turns and looks at me like I'm an invasive species.

She has never liked me, and I'm regretting not wearing the white dress after all. As the organ strikes up, my stomach fills with granite. What am I doing? What am I imagining I'm capable of? What will people say when I carry out my plan? He has her and when today is over, nothing will make a difference any more. Not for me and not for them.

Then she arrives, walking up the aisle, slowly, with her father. Her gaze rests on him, waiting by the steps up to the altar. She touches a blood red rose in her bouquet. Red roses and baby's-breath. I reach into my handbag and clench what's inside, what I put there. I feel the pain as it cuts into my palm. Feel the blood trickle. It feels good. For a moment I wonder if I will be able to do it.

I first met him on Tinder, three years ago. And then at a mutual friend's party. The house was by a lake. It was summer. I saw him when I rounded the corner to the veranda. Dark hair, grey-blue clear eyes, light coloured, turned-up jeans, a white T-shirt with a dark jacket, white trainers. He was beautiful.

I had fallen in love with the idea of him long before that party. I neglected to make myself known to him straight away. Instead I sat and studied him for a while, from a distance. The wonky smile, pointy canines, his eyes when he was talking to someone, his fingers as he drew them through his dark fringe. He drank little and flirted even less with the many girls hanging off him. It surprised me just as much as it pleased me to see him looking for someone... for me.

The pipe-organ's last note is hanging in the room as we sit down. A few people clear their throats but no one speaks. There is a kind of tension in the air. I lean my head against the wooden panelling as my pulse thumps as if possessed in my carotid artery. I try to calm down by closing my eyes and breathing in through my nose. I want to find his scent, but I can't, it's too long ago. Just one year and already he's here, and it's him and her, not us.

I smell church pews and singed electric heaters, I smell old woodwork and tallow, but not him or the cologne he used every day. I turn my thoughts inwards until I find us together.

When I open my eyes, the woman is standing at the altar rail. She bows her head and buries her nose in blood red petals. Red roses and baby's-breath. He used to buy them for me. It was me who taught him that combination will make women do almost anything.

The woman whispers something in the ear of a friend, or perhaps a sister, before she passes her the bouquet. As new notes seep out into the room, she turns to him. She rests her eyes there for a long time before she surveys the nave like a ship's captain.

Her gaze is steady. It's clear that the occasion is thought through and prepared down to the smallest detail. Not lavish as I would have had it, but 'less is more' as it's called. She hasn't planned this alone. I can see where he's left his mark. They have spent time on this together. The impersonal ceremony, the way the church is decorated and the simple dress she is wearing. It's not unlike the one he gave me. That's how he likes it. The realisation makes me unexpectedly happy.

I cut myself on what's lying in my handbag. I start to doubt that I can really do this, quickly looking around. Maybe I should just leave them in peace? Regardless, it's too late now.

At last she lets go of her father's hand and as she does so, she wavers. The first sign that she is moved, that this means something.

Her family are for the most part unknown to me. Some faces I have seen before, but none of them know me or our story. For them I'm the other; the ex. His family on the other hand, were like an extension of my own. I can identify them from behind, one by one. His sister with long, dark hair. His brothers next to her. His mother, who was going to be my mother-in-law forever. She nodded when she saw me under the tree outside.

The priest climbs down the three steps from the altar and greets the closest family members, as if he wants to thank them for coming. The he turns to the altarpiece depicting Jesus and two women; Virgin Mary or Mary Magdalene? I don't know. They lie at the feet of the saviour. He rests his hand on the head of one, the other looks away.

The recessional song is impersonal, I would have hired a live performer. A song that would have made everyone cry, or smile though tears. Maybe 'Faded' by Alan Walker or 'Perfect' by Ed Sheeran.

But it's not our ceremony. She is the director. I'm just an extra, cheeky enough to show up.

I don't have the energy the listen. The words are not my concern. Not until they start to leave do I raise my eyes and stand up. The procession is slow. The woman controls the pace, takes her time, looks people in the eye and smiles a Mona Lisa smile. She walks slowly, as if she wants the moment to last forever. The others follow, row by row the church empties.

It takes a long time until the back row is to join in, and I feel like an idiot who has taken a wrong turn and ended up in the middle of the pitch in front of a packed stadium. When I arrived this seemed like a good hiding place. Now everyone is heading straight for me. As she passes, I steel myself and meet her eye, while I squeeze what's in my bag, tight. I pull my hand up. Suck blood from my finger, while I'm confused to see neither hate or anger in her eyes, not sympathy either. It makes me angry.

She disappears out the door. The others follow. I can't bear to be here any more, so I squeeze into the queue of black suits, bow my head, but still notice the accusatory looks from those who are sure I shouldn't be here, and definitely not this close to the head of the procession. So be it. I can't bear to sit on that subs' bench any more. Besides, in this game, all the possible substitutions have been made already.

A man snorts loudly as he squeezes by me in the porch. I lose my balance in my high heels. Another man, one of his best friends, steadies me and mumbles something, before he disappears out into the churchyard. I clench my teeth and kick off the heels and place them carefully in my handbag. I check in on what's lying in there already. The handbag is far too big for this sort of occasion but I needed the room.

With my shoes off I plant my feet on the cold wooden floor, painted grey. It strikes me that the church must have been built directly on the ground. It's as if black mould is rising up through the old, rotting wood and is threatening to suck me in and cover me with damp, black soil. I pull my suit jacket closer and feel a tightening in my throat.

Then the tears come. They are violent and shut out the air. Ashamed, I look down at the hefty slate flagstones as I emerge onto the church steps. I sense, more than see, the sympathetic looks. There are many. I feel a terrible loneliness as I walk through the crowd and continue on between unknown gravestones, as if I'm here with another purpose. A sharp stone cuts into the pad if my foot and eases the pain inside me. I need to get away.

All at once a powerful hand lands on my shoulder. I turn around. It's his brother. He puts his arm around me.

'It's good to see you,' he says.

'You too,' I sob. Confused, I lean into him for a short moment, totally aware that people are now staring at me even more. They see me imposing on his family, and on a day like this. A day when she should lay claim to all the attention. I want to pull away but he holds me tight.

'Some people tear pages out of their lives, as if they have never been written,' he says. 'But you have let them stay in place, unedited. That's good. There are no chapters missing. Come!'

I follow him as he weaves through the crowd, holding my hand tightly as if he is afraid that I will escape. The grass feels softer under my feet. My pulse beats steadily in my head. I understand where he's taking me, but does he know what's in my bag? Does he know my plan?

139

People move out of the way, create space. At first they are blurry shadows, then their faces become sharp. His mother, sister, his old uncle with bright white hair who always enjoyed a chat. His aunt who thought I was a poor choice.

Then we stop. His brother steps aside. The woman is standing with her back to us. Then she turns towards me, as if she's picked up my scent. Without uttering a word she makes room for me. It strikes me that she wants to give us a moment alone. That she thinks I deserve it, despite everything.

I let go of his brother's hand. The others disappear before me as I stare at the white wood, a cinema screen on which a blurry black and white film flickers.

He came back with the white dress, now at home, hanging in the window, waving goodbye. Courage failed me. I didn't dare to wear it today. I see him as he lowers himself onto knee and holds the ring up in front of me. 'Yours forever.' I see us together day after day as we, like eager yellowhammers, build our nest on the ground and decorate it with the finest straw, while planning the rest of our lives together. The rest of our lives. Then the film is over and all I see white. It was so beautiful, so right, so ours... and now.

Once more I collapse, inwardly. The unbearable feeling of when he left. Everything that can't be repaired. There is absolutely nothing I can do. The feeling of losing control of my whole being. The hopelessness. Even if I were to move a mountain or fetch a star, he's never coming back to me.

I draw my engagement ring off my ring finger and hold it for a moment, twist and turn it, try to read the engraving, but can't manage it through the tears. I don't need to see it. I open my handbag and first take out my shoes and step into them. Then I fish out what's been lying in my bag. A red petal falls to the ground as I thread my engagement ring onto three rose stems and a spray of baby's-breath. I lean forwards, stretch out my my hand and throw three red roses onto the white coffin and whisper something only he can hear.

Afterwards I turn, with my eyes I search the crowd. Walk towards her and give her a hug.

'Thank you for coming!' she says.

ABOUT THE AUTHOR

Agnes Lovise Matre (born 1966) is a Norwegian author who comes from Haugesund, a city on the south west coast of Norway. She is best known for her crime books.

To wait

Prableen Kaur Aa Vente

Translated from Norwegian by Nancy Langfeldt

I regret it. I should have worn the woollen tights. Then I wouldn't be shivering now. These flimsy H&M tights are pointless, even if they are 200 denier, when it's minus ten degrees. If Sarah could see this she would say that I ought to put on more clothes, that I don't wear enough layers. Wool is best, she would have nagged. I would have laughed and said yeah, yeah, mum!

Henrik should have been here fifteen minutes ago. He hasn't texted or rung to let me know and I don't dare ask where he's at. I hate this feeling. When I know what I want, and know that it's not dangerous or wrong, but I don't dare to do it. I don't dare to make plans. I don't dare to order my food in a restaurant. I don't dare to ask for help in a shop. I can walk round a shop several times, looking at completely uninteresting things. Feel the fabrics, check which materials the clothes are made of, just to woman up to asking a question. I do it even though the shop assistants have asked me if they can help with anything. It's like my mouth won't open. Like someone with a needle and thread has stitched it shut with many, many tiny stitches. It's like I don't have words, language or punctuation left. It's ironic that I'm actually quite brave even though I don't dare to do simple things. Like I can suddenly put my hand up at school and say something, despite not knowing if I'm right or wrong. I can talk to strangers on the bus or at the post office. But asking Henrik if he'll be here soon, that I can't do. I don't want to bother him, or do something that makes him change his mind and decide not to meet up with me after all. I think it's better to be calm and fit in with whatever suits him. If I do that, then I won't be in the way. I can't ruin anything.

Compared to other people, I'm small. I'm scared of being a bother, being difficult. Not good enough, I don't want to do anything which might mean I'm rejected in favour of someone else. I'd rather hold back. I keep my frustrations to myself. I make myself into the person other people want me to be.

The first time I noticed Henrik was at the school Christmas assembly. He was wearing a dark suit and a white shirt. His top button was open, and I remember thinking that he had to become my boyfriend one day. I just knew straight away, I'm going to do everything for that guy.

He'd walked up to the microphone, adjusted the stand for his height and suddenly the microphone fell on the floor. Everyone started laughing and I got stressed. I didn't want him to embarrass himself in front of the whole school and all the parents. But he picked up the microphone and started speaking as if nothing had happened. He didn't seem nervous, he didn't stumble on his words. He didn't say errr or ummm. He was totally unaffected. I wish I was like that or could be like him, someone who didn't get spooked or let anything ruffle their feathers.

When everyone had finished performing I went over to speak to him. I said I thought he was really, really clever and brave. He smiled and said thank you, that no one had ever said something so nice to him before. I don't know if I quite believed that, but I really wanted it to be true, that I would be special enough for him. Afterwards I got such a stomach ache from talking to him that I ran to the toilet. I put the lid down and sat there until the pins and needles in my palms, fingers, legs, feet, stomach and heart passed.

He was in the same year as me but we didn't get to know each other until we met at a party a few years later. We ended up talking the whole night and when the party was over he walked me home. We met up the next day. We went for a walk. Then several months passed.

I didn't hear from him at all but then he sent me a text, totally out of the blue. He asked how it was going and if I would like to go to the cinema. We went to the cinema and then met up again two days later. We hung out at the playground in front of my parents' house. We swung on the swings, got sand in our shoes and under our nails. Short and intense, but sporadic. Again and again. He had kind of taken hold of me, without actually holding me and I didn't want to give up.

I'm not wearing wool socks either. I can feel my toes getting colder and colder. Stiffer. Maybe they are starting to go a bit red? You know that feeling when you've been outside in the winter? Around Christmas or something, with your family? Then you get back to the cabin after a long day skiing and take off your socks, and when you touch your toes the skin goes white when you press it. And when you relieve the pressure it goes red again. I think my toes are like that right now. I try and move them. Curl them up in my shoes, but it's getting harder.

The tip of my nose is red. I try and pull faces to move my nose. Warm it up a bit. I put my hands in my pockets. My fingers slide over the cold metal of my keys, the plastic of my lipbalm against my palm, and the hard case of my credit card holder. There is nothing I can use to blow my nose and I don't want to do it on the arms of my jumper or jacket. I sniff at even intervals. I suck the snot back and upwards in my nose.

I don't want to look at the people passing by. I just look down. At my shoes. I need to move around a bit. I gather a little snow mound in front of me with my shoes. I use my feet to drag it towards the centre and make the mound bigger. To finish I make a little snow tower. Then I carefully pat down the top of the tower with the soles of my shoes, which leave an imprint.

I pretend I'm dancing inside myself. I make little moves under my jacket that no one else can see. It's pretty cool, because only I know what I'm doing. Everyone else thinks I'm just standing here, hanging out. But I'm dancing. I tense the muscles in my arms, move my fingers, move my stomach, just about manage to move my toes.

It starts to hurt. I'm not enjoying it anymore, standing out here, but I like pain. It means I'm feeling something. I don't understand why I have to stand here. I could wait indoors, but I feel like I deserve to be outside, it's my punishment for something, I'm not quite sure what. Or am I giving too much of myself now? Of my time? He clearly doesn't respect it, if he did he'd be here by now. He would have been in touch. He was the one who wanted to meet up. I have a boyfriend now. It's not like it was before, and I know Henrik well. We have tried before and it didn't work. I should be at home tidying or spending time with my boyfriend, but I said I was free, because I want to see Henrik. I just give everything I have. I remember how things were, before. I would make us dinner, book cinema tickets, queue up to get into the theatre or wait for him at the bowling alley. Then he would send a text saying that he couldn't make it after all, and I would say that's fine, we can do something another day. I carry on giving, he takes my time and I let him. Maybe it's not his fault? I'm the one who can't set boundaries, fence myself off. Build a wall. Look after myself. I let him do the same thing over again.

Can I limit how much I give away? Do I have any guarantees he won't leave me again? That he doesn't want to be my person? He has to stay with me. Be mine. That's what I want. Really. That's why I'm standing here now, feeling my body getting more and more numb. He's the one I want to text when I trip on the stairs and face-plant or when I get a job interview at a café. He's the one I want to call when it hurts to breathe. Won't all this disappear if I set some boundaries? I think so, because I've never tried anything else, and I don't think it's a good idea either. Every person has individual characteristics. This is mine. I give. I have, after all, lived with myself for some years, so this I know. He takes my time without giving anything in return and I let him. I don't stop meeting him. Don't stop calling him. Don't stop texting. I don't stop lacing my fingers through his the few times we meet. I do all these things even though I know that he won't give enough back, but then I think that maybe it is enough for me. That there isn't more. That halfway is enough, because I don't deserve any more.

I raise my shoulders to warm my ears with my scarf. Oh, I've been here for twenty-five minutes now. I pace a couple of steps back and forth. Jump some pretend jumps. Maybe we should end this now. This waiting, hoping. We've done it many times. Or I have done it many times. He gets in

148

touch and I drop everything. I hope that this time it will work, this time he will become my life. Not temporarily, but permanently. I look down the street. I consider if I should go home. End this before it starts again. I take a few steps but then I see him walking towards me. I want to go over there. Meet him halfway, but I stay where I am. He doesn't deserve it. He can come to me.

He gives me a hug and I want him to hold me tighter so that I can defrost. He is sorry that he's late. He promises it won't happen again. This time he really means it, he says. I say that it's fine, it doesn't matter. 'I hope you haven't been waiting out here for a long time,' he says.

'No, no. I was a bit late myself.'

ABOUT THE AUTHOR

Prableen Kaur is a Norwegian author who was born in Lørenskog, a suburb of Oslo, in 1993. She made her literary debut in 2012 with the publication of the biographical work *Jeg er Prableen (I am Prableen)*. Her first novel, titled *Ferdig med ting (Finished with matters)* was published in 2018. She studied law at the University of Oslo and is an active participant in public debates, both as an engaged individual and as a politician representing Arbeiderpartiet, Norway's largest socialist party. In 2011 she was named Norwegian of the Year.

The End of the World

Bjørn Sortland

Translated from Norwegian by Nancy Langfeldt

Markus joined the class three months ago. He and his family come from Manglerud in Oslo. 'They're from the capital, no less, the capital,' says Dad.

Dad doesn't like people from the capital. He says they are full of themselves and that they don't know anything about people outside of the city.

'All of us, living out here on the west coast, we keep this country going, people from Oslo...' Dad says, 'They wander around the forest in lifejackets picking mushrooms. They are complete idiots.'

It's true, Markus is a bit different. But he doesn't wander around the forest in a lifejacket picking mushrooms.

His dad is a priest and they have just moved here. I don't know what Markus does when he's not at school, but I would like to find out. He's sort of more grown up than the rest of us in year nine, he answers politely, says smart things to the teachers. For example, does he have a girlfriend in Manglerud? Actually that's not something I want to know anything about.

Every part of me is in love with him. My heart, my brain, my whole head, my stomach, yes, my whole body. My brain says I'm not allowed to speak to him because I'll just make a fool of myself. But my legs are in love with him, so at lunch break on Thursday I go over to where he usually hangs out, over by the old football goal.

'Hi,' I say.

'Hi,' he says.

My mouth is dry.

'I am... very worried,' I say in a strange voice, my tongue stuck fast to the side of my mouth. 'About the climate. I am worried about the melting icecaps, floods and nuclear war and the end of the world. And all that. Kind of.'

Blah-blah-blah.

Cringe, cringe, cringe.

'I don't like science fiction,' says Markus. 'But now and again I think about what it would be like to arrive here, in the present day, from, for example, the Viking era, and see what we're up to. They would be shocked at all the stuff we are destroying and polluting.'

'Yes! I have had the exact same thought!' I say, realising that I sound far too eager. 'And all the light and noise pollution, ski jumps and dance music all night long!' I say. 'They are ruining the earth.'

I babble away, someone could at least step in and shut me up. But I steam ahead, who knows when I will next dare to speak to him.

'I'm afraid of all sorts, for example I dread speaking in lessons,' I say, moving as close to him as I dare. 'We were supposed to give presentations on a topic of our choice last year but I didn't have to because I have anxiety.' I say abruptly. 'I thought I'd talk about something to do with these changes in the world,' I say. 'But, like, I don't know where to start. So I need some help. I thought maybe you could help me, because I'm so damn nervous about public speaking that I can't do it. I nearly throw up when I get up in front of the class. I'm about to get epilepsy. It's so embarrassing, I'll die.' I say.

Wow!

My brain is incredibly impressed. This is all lies. We don't have to do presentations.

'So maybe you could, like, listen to my presentation first, in advance,' I say. 'I could practise on you a bit first, then it might get sort of easier.'

Practise on you. Like that's a smart thing to say?

'Oh?' Markus asks.

'It's just that,' I say quickly. 'Like I said, I didn't dare do it last year. So I have to do it this year. Everyone else did it already,' I lie.

What am I saying? My brain just invented all this just now.

'OK. If you think I can help, sure,' says Markus.

He doesn't sound as enthusiastic as I want him to be. Is that hesitation? No. I can't think about that now.

'Do you have time after school on Friday?' I ask.

'Friday... You mean tomorrow? It's Thursday today,' Markus says, his breath smelling like apples.

'Yes,' I say, in a very low, proper, newscaster voice. 'Tomorrow.'

All Thursday evening I sit in my room. I am so in love that I can only drink cola. I don't sleep at all that night, maybe just for one and a half hours. Then I get up early and shower, using up all the warm water. Mum says we shouldn't shower so much, that we're destroying the natural oils on our skin. But if there is something not to give a damn about today, it is the natural oils on our skin. I put on my make up so that it looks like I'm not wearing make up, wear a good perfume, just a little on my neck, wear my best clothes but make it look like I'm not trying too hard. Phew. It's tough.

The day at school passes normally. Almost. At least I can't see anything different about Markus. He looks like he might have forgotten the whole thing, but who knows, you can't really tell what Markus is thinking by looking at him. I bet it has something to do with Oslo and Manglerud.

When the last lesson (P.E.) is over, I wait at the school gates. I have my rucksack on and gym bag in hand. And a racing pulse. A bit.

I needed some sort of plan, so during lunch break I went Eilef's Bookshop sale. There is always a sale at Eilef's Bookshop. Especially on books, even though they have almost no books there, just cards and games and fridge magnets. My stomach rumbles, but I didn't have time to eat anything, just to drink a cola.

I showered super quick after P.E., didn't dry my hair or put on my make up. So I'm waiting with soaking wet hair, probably looking like a drowned cat.

At last Markus appears. He has combed his newly showered hair in a kind of dumb way, it looks a bit old fashioned – but he is still cool. He smells good. Apple shampoo.

We head home. It's awkward. I don't know what to talk about, so I kick the gravel a bit – to look cool. Except it's not actually gravel. It's just asphalt, so there I am kicking the air, looking like a floppy puppet gone bananas. When we get in to our hallway, I quickly drag Markus down to the basement living room. I don't want Mum to discover him.

'Aren't we going to take off our shoes...'

'No, we always wear our shoes indoors in our house, wellies, spikes, ski boots... Don't sweat it.'

Suddenly I kind of see our house anew. With Markus' eyes. It's probably very different from Manglerud in Oslo.

I sniff and yes, it smells a bit of fish, even though we haven't eaten that for dinner for several days. And it's a bit old-fashioned in here, not like the houses in the blogs and magazines that Mum reads, we have leaded,

155

coloured glass in the door down to the basement. It's probably not like Markus' house in Oslo either.

'So what precisely is the topic of your presentation?'

'Precisely? The end of the world,' I say, realising I've left the book up in the hallway.

'Yes, but...'

'There are lots of different theories,' I say. 'I have a book. Wait a minute.'

I run upstairs.

'Hallo! I'll be right down with pizza,' says Mum from the kitchen. 'Do you have a boy round? You were so quiet and rushed downstairs, I thought I heard an extra pair of feet. And a boy's voice?'

'We don't want pizza,' I say quickly. 'Markus is allergic to... tomatoes. Everything to do with tomatoes, tomato purée and, and all possible types of tomato sauce.'

Ouch, I should never have mentioned his name!

'Oh,' says Mum. 'I say, a *boy*. Markus. Mmm. But it's Friday, pizza-day. It's not often you have boy visits in the basement.'

'He is definitely not hungry, we ate on our way home, we had a hot-dog at Ove's,' I say.

Mum looks disappointed. That's how it's got to be, I can't take the chance, she is a terrible cook. Once, she made pizza with carrots and peas on it. For my birthday. Frozen ones.

I run into the bathroom and look in the mirror; yes, I look like a scared and pale cat. But it's too late for make up now. I panic and put some of Mum's lipstick on. And regret it. It just leaves me with a very, very red line on my white face. White and red. The Red Cross. Strawberries and cream. The apple and Snow White. (Or was that Sleeping Beauty?)

I try to wipe it off, it doesn't go well, I look like the Joker in Batman. I don't dare to get it off properly, because the longer I faff about here, the bigger the risk that Mum goes down to the basement with something or other for Markus. Whatever she has hurriedly whipped up without any tomatoes. My stomach rumbles. I've drunk too much cola. I feel sick.

I run down to the basement.

'Here's the book,' I say. '*Millennium Prophecies* by Stephen Skinner. *Predictions for the year 2000 and beyond from the world's greatest seers and mystics*,' I read. 'It was on sale.'

I give the big book to Markus. It has a big green eye on the front which is covering the whole globe. The cover looks like the packaging for a computer game. I might have spent too short a time in Eilef's Bookshop.

'Hmm,' says Markus, who has sat down on our red sofa. He leans forward and starts reading.

I sit alongside him, almost touching. Almost.

I get a terrible urge to leave over and smell his neck, not kiss, no, no. Just smell.

Apple shampoo. Apple-boyneck.

'Seems like there are a lot of different theories in here,' says Markus.

157

'Yes,' I say. 'There are like, loads.'

'And there isn't much information about any of them.'

'But all the most important theories are in there, aren't they?' I say, with what I hope is a soft voice.

'Yes, I guess so, I'm not familiar with all of it. What do you need my help with?'

Markus looks at me with very very blue eyes, I shift a bit on the sofa. Imagine, he is here. With me, in the basement sitting room. Just us two. Woohoo. This might go well.

'I need help... choosing something,' I say. 'As you noticed, there are a lot of theories presented. I won't have time to talk about all of them. I don't know really. Do you have any suggestions?' I ask.

'No, I'm not too sure. It has to be your own work.'

Mortifying pause.

'I want to talk about the end of the world, Judgement Day, all the things I'm afraid of. That polar bears are going to be extinct. That the whales are full of plastic. About floods and nuclear war. Do you think about it?' I ask.

'It's been raining non-stop for a month now,' says Markus. 'That sort of thing makes me worried. The weather in Vestlandet is almost like in the story of Noah in the Bible...'

'Hi,' says Mum, who suddenly, totally coincidentally, is standing in the doorway. 'I've experimented a bit and made some cheese sandwiches for you. I put ketchup on yours, Therese. But yours don't have any,' says Mum, winking at Markus. 'We don't want you getting ill from coming to visit us.'

'Mum!' I say.

'That sounds great,' says Markus, smiling at Mum. But he looks a bit uncertain.

'Enjoy yourselves,' says Mum. 'And remember that there is more to life than homework. Be careful of the tomatoes! LOL!'

She winks on her way out.

LOL! Seriously?

It gets very quiet when Mum leaves.

Then it happens. My stomach grumbles. So incredibly embarrassing.

And it doesn't just grumble.

Suddenly I let out a proper fart. A giant fart that won't stop. All that carbon dioxide in the cola wants to escape right now.

Markus looks at me with those blue eyes. And smiles, shyly.

I don't manage to say anything.

So that what it feels like to die. It's much worse than I thought.

Markus pretends nothing has happened, he is very polite, but that's surely something he's learned from his priest-mum and priest-dad in Oslo.

The room stinks.

I try to eat, but it's too late, everything is too late now. The world is ending. And the cheese sandwiches smell like poo. Swiss cheese melted over a mixture of tuna fish and onion.

Markus will never return to giant-fart-girl with the Joker lipstick and her psycho tuna-fish mum.

Well, now the whole world can just end, get destroyed by the melting icecaps and floods, and then the whole thing can finish with a quick and painless nuclear war.

'Do you sometimes miss the capital?' I ask.

ABOUT THE AUTHOR

Bjørn Sortland is a Norwegian author who was born in Bergen in 1968. He grew up in the town of Sortland on the island of Bømlo, off the south west coast of Norway. He has written 60 books across a variety of genres, for children, young adults and adults. The books have been published widely in many different countries, including Turkey, Hungary, Bulgaria, South Korea, USA, Taiwan, Scandinavia, Egypt and Palestine. He also writes for theatre and film.

EXPLANATORY NOTE ON ALL
THE NORWEGIAN STORIES

We chose authors who have run creative workshops at our schools to write these stories. We asked some of the students involved in these workshops and it was their idea to use these authors, because they liked them and their books and especially the stories they had told during the workshops. The students wanted stories about young love.

A Frameful of Memories

Constança Freire de Sousa, in collaboration with students from Emídio Navarro Secondary School

Translated from Portuguese by Beth Fowler

'**W**hat do you mean?' Miguel asked the nurse, his heart racing.

'A free room came up so we moved your grandma into a single. At the end of the corridor on the right.' She pointed the way.

Miguel took a deep breath. When the nurse had told him his grandma's file wasn't in the usual place, Miguel had thought something terrible must have happened to her. But now he pressed on quietly down the corridor towards his grandma's new room.

163

The corridor was as bleak and silent as the rest of the building. It was painted in chilly shades of grey and blue, like the sea on a stormy day. As he walked, Miguel glanced through the rectangular windows into each room. Some had the curtain drawn across, but others didn't and through these Miguel could see the residents of each room. They were all very elderly, sitting, hunched, on armchairs or lying in bed. A great wave of sadness swept through him him when he looked inside the rooms and sensed all those lives that were long, but tired, ancient and alone.

It was a relief to reach Grandma's room. Miguel opened the door and went in, pulling it shut behind him. The room was filled with warm sunlight coming through the window, diffusing through the room. Miguel took in the long bed, the wardrobe in the corner, its door ajar, the bedside table and, finally, his eyes settled on Grandma. She was sitting in the armchair next to the bed, turned to face the window, welcoming the sun. Her white hair shone, almost dazzling in the golden light. She seemed like a soft, white cloud. In her hand, she was tenderly clutching the silver picture frame that Miguel's mum had given her.

Miguel went over to her.

'Hi, Grandma!'

He gave her a light kiss on the wrinkly forehead that was, still, as soft as a baby's skin. He inhaled that scent that was unique to her. Grandma smelt of roses. Or was it lavender? She smelt of flowers, anyway. Miguel didn't know anything about flowers. But he knew that Grandma always smelt good.

'Grandma?' Miguel called. He pulled a chair over from the corner of the room, placed his backpack on the floor and sat down. 'Grandma, look at me.'

Several seconds passed before she raised her head. Her eyes had been blue, a strong, shining blue, impenetrable, unique. Now they had lost much of their strength. They were milky eyes, tired and, sadly, vacant.

'Do you know who I am?'

Grandma didn't reply. She just looked at him as though looking through him.

'I'm Miguel, your grandson. I'm Ana's son. Grandma, it's me.'

Slowly, Miguel prised the frame from her hands. The photograph inside was of a two-storey house, painted yellow and with a red tile veranda all the way round. In the window of the first floor you could see a dog's nose and propped up against the main door were a rusty rake and a watering can. In one corner of the photo you could see part of a giant tyre, which Miguel knew belonged to his grandfather's ancient green tractor. He could remember the time, when he was still a little boy, when he hid in the back of the tractor, amongst the crates, and went with his grandfather to the field. He smiled nostalgically as he remembered how Grandpa had nearly eaten him alive when he found him.

'Let's think about something else, Grandma, so that you aren't always staring at this photo. Would you like me to read to you?'

The old lady nodded her head almost imperceptibly. Miguel carefully placed the frame on the bedside table and pulled a book from his backpack. It was a collection of poems by Alberto Caeiro, whom Grandma had loved when she was young. Miguel opened the book at the page where he had stopped on his last visit and started to read.

'When springtime comes,
If I've already died,
The flowers will bloom just the same
And the trees will be no less green than they were last spring.
Reality has no need of me.
It gives me great joy to think
That my death has no importance whatsoever.
If I knew I'd die tomorrow
And spring came the day after,
I'd die happy, because it came the day after.
If this is its time, why wouldn't it come?
I like everything to be real and everything to be right;
And I like it because that's the way it would be
even if I didn't like it.
That's why, if I die now, I'll die happy,
Because everything is real and everything is right.'

He stopped before the final stanza when, in the corner of his eye, he caught a movement from Grandma's armchair. He looked up. Grandma had picked up the frame again. Her eyes, there was no doubting it, were filled with love.

'I'd die happy...' whispered Grandma.

Miguel didn't like to be confronted with the loss of his grandmother. But she had always been very clear and objective when it came to her own death. At least while her memory allowed. And, being realistic, Miguel knew that Grandma wouldn't last forever. Now he found himself striving to draw out the words she had to say to him.

'What do you need, Grandma? To...' He tried to say the words 'die happy', but his voice failed him.

His grandmother seemed to read in silence the words he hadn't said. She turned the frame towards Miguel, showing him the farmhouse. And, for a few seconds, Miguel felt that his grandmother knew exactly who he was, who she herself was, where she was and what she needed. He saw a whole life within her gaze. And he felt that he liked her even more when he saw her like this. They smiled at each other.

Then his mobile rang, Miguel said goodbye with another kiss on the forehead, whispered 'I love you' in Grandma's ear and crossed the corridor towards the exit, where his mother was waiting for him in the car. Before he walked out of the grey doors, Miguel glanced back and thought to himself: 'I have to take Grandma to the farm, no matter what.'

The following Wednesday, Miguel's mum came to pick him up at school and dropped him in front of his grandmother's nursing home, as usual. Miguel spent the whole journey thinking about Grandma, the farm, the house and the photograph. His mum parked the car and pulled her mobile out of her handbag. Before he got out, Miguel plucked up the courage.

'Mum?'

'Mhmm?' His mum didn't raise her eyes from the mobile.

'Do you think that one of these days we could... Could we take Grandma to the farm?'

She took a moment to react, as if his words had travelled a long distance before being processed. She lowered the phone.

'To the farm? Miguel, you know that the farm doesn't belong to her anymore.'

'Yes, but we could ask Alice and Mario if we can visit, seeing as you're frien...'

Mum interrupted him.

'We're not taking Grandma out of the home. She isn't well enough, either physically or mentally. She wouldn't appreciate it, honey, or even realise we were there!'

'Oh, Mum, but I'm sure...'

'Miguel. Don't insist. I wish we could take Grandma out and about. But she isn't... She isn't really her.' Mum ran her hands through her hair and looked at the nursing home with a mixture of fear and sadness. Then she snapped back to her usual self, practical and energetic. 'I'll come and get you in an hour. Behave yourself!'

Miguel got out of the car feeling extremely disappointed. He had suspected that his mum would react that way.

The biggest problem with this refusal was that Miguel couldn't take Grandma out of the home without the authorisation of the adult responsible for her: his mother. Even if Miguel had a car and was old enough to drive – which he wasn't, he still had a few years to go – he couldn't take Grandma any further than the café on the corner without his mother's signature. Or his uncle's. But Miguel didn't like his uncle, he was brutish and said nasty things and, worst of all, he never came to visit Grandma. Asking him for help was out of the question.

He walked down the corridor towards the room still thinking about his possibilities. And, in all honesty, he was starting to think he didn't have any. But he loved his grandma so much that he couldn't bear the idea of failing. She wanted to go to the farm and Miguel would take her there, even if he had to carry her!

When he entered the room, Miguel found his grandma in her usual armchair, with Amanda arranging a blanket over her legs. Amanda was the nurse assigned to her. Miguel often came across her in the corridors and in Grandma's room and was very fond of her. Amanda had bright green eyes and a big, genuine smile, full of white teeth. She was slim and delicate and Miguel thought that there was no one in the world better suited to caring for the elderly.

'Miguel!' exclaimed Amanda. Then she turned to Grandma. 'See how lucky you are? A grandson who visits every week is just wonderful!'

'Hello Amanda,' replied Miguel, returning her smile.

'Hi, Grandma!'

This time Grandma smiled at him. But she immediately twisted her body in her chair to reach for the frame on the bedside table.

'Wait, I'll get you your photo.' Amanda passed the frame to Grandma and turned to Miguel. She said in a low voice:

'She's been much better today. She used words and everything. But every now and then she remembers and asks for the frame. Does the house in the photo still exist?'

'Yes, it does, but it isn't ours anymore.'

'Have you thought about taking her there? I think it might give her some peace.' Amanda's eyes were wide and serious.

'My mum doesn't want to take her...' Miguel averted his eyes from Amanda's. He was embarrassed that even the nurse had realised the importance of the farm when his mother hadn't.

'Tell your mum that we have special vans to take her in. We just need her signature and we'll take care of the rest.' Amanda's voice was friendly and Miguel felt he could raise his eyes again.

'I'll tell her. Thanks.'

Amanda left and Miguel was alone with Grandma. He looked at her, so small in her armchair, the frame in her hands, staring. All of a sudden, their trip to Disneyland a few years ago popped into his mind. He remembered how they had been sitting together on that huge rollercoaster, Space Mountain. He remembered how he had been afraid, how he had thought that as soon as the train turned upside down he would slip out of the safety harness and end up spread-eagled on the ground. He remembered how Grandma took his hand, smiled at him with that smile that was hers alone, and said in his ear: 'As long as I'm here, nothing bad is going to happen to you. And I think we're going to have a lot of fun.'

Miguel placed a finger under her chin and raised her head so that they were looking right at one another. In his grandmother's eyes there was nothing but gentleness. Miguel suddenly felt like crying.

'You protected me, I'll protect you. I'm still going to take you to the farm, Grandma. I promise.'

The next time Miguel went to the home, he was determined. He was going to speak to the manager and find out how he was going to get his grandma out of there without his mother's signature. He marched along the corridors until he reached the door he knew must be the right one. He knocked and went in.

Miguel hadn't even opened his mouth and he already knew it wasn't worth it. The manager was a strict, severe woman, her hair pulled tightly back over the top of her head. She had rectangular glasses that sat halfway down her nose and thin, tight lips, so small that Miguel thought it must be impossible for her to smile. He stammered out a false explanation about how his mother had asked him to go out with Grandma in the home's vehicle, but she had forgotten to leave a signature before she left for work.

171

'No one leaves the home without a form signed by the responsible adult,' replied the woman on the other side of the desk, without looking at him. 'Wait for your mother to come back.'

Miguel wanted to insist, but he didn't really know how to deal with a woman as scathing and indifferent as this. When he opened his mouth to speak, the manager looked up and stared at him over the top of her glasses.

'No one leaves the home without a form signed by the responsible adult,' she repeated, before Miguel could say anything else.

'R-right. So I'll ask her to sign it.' Miguel was dying to get out of there.

'Do you have the form?'

'Wh-what?' asked Miguel, hand already on the door handle.

'The form, the form!' scolded the woman impatiently. 'Take this one, this is what has to be filled in and signed.'

Miguel took the sheet from her, murmured an almost inaudible 'thanks' and ran out. Back in Grandma's room, he exhaled in relief. He needed another solution. But for now, it was time to spend a while with Grandma.

He had only read one poem when Amanda came into the room.

'Hi Miguel!' she said in her usual friendly voice. 'I've come to see if your grandma wants to go to the café. She hasn't left her room today and the weather's nice, I think it'll do her good. Shall we?'

Miguel agreed. He helped Amanda put Grandma's coat on and then held one of her arms while Amanda took the other. They walked down the corridor like that, joined like a chain. Only when they were in the street did Miguel think of another solution.

'Amanda, is there any way to take Grandma to the house in the photo without my mum's signature?'

Amanda looked at him doubtfully. Miguel hurriedly explained:

'She went off to work and forgot to sign!' he lied.

'No, Miguel, no one is authorised to do that. And if I did it for you, I'd lose my job.' Amanda thought for a second in silence. 'But I'm happy that your mum has agreed. There's no hurry, we can wait for her to come back and ask her to sign. When does she get back?'

'Tomorrow,' he improvised, his chest tight with all the lies.

Amanda smiled at him. They walked on to the café, where they had tea with Grandma, and returned to the home with their arms linked. Before he left, Miguel hugged his grandma. In her ear, he told her how much he loved her. Grandma squeezed him tightly and Miguel could sense everything she wasn't able to say to him. At that moment he was more determined than ever that they had to go to the farm. And now Miguel had a plan that would work.

The next time Miguel went to the home, he was clutching the signed form in his hand. His insides were in such a frenzy, it was though an electric current was running through his blood, a tingling that consumed every inch of skin. The previous day he had searched in the bottom of his backpack for an authorisation slip for a school field trip, signed by his mother. He had put the piece of paper on his desk, with the form on top, and had carefully traced the signature. Miguel felt so guilty that he hadn't been able to look his mother in the eye since he did it. He knew perfectly well that forging a signature wasn't just wrong but also illegal. He had broken the law. But Grandma didn't have much time and she was the priority.

The first thing Miguel did was to go and speak with Amanda, who was very happy to learn that they could finally take Grandma to the farm. Then he went to hand the form to the manager. The frightening woman peered at him over the top of her glasses for a few seconds, then inspected the form. Miguel held his breath until he heard her say:

'This all seems to be in order.'

Then he murmured a 'thank you' and ran out to tell Amanda and Grandma. They were both in the room. Miguel burst in, all smiles.

'That's it! Grandma! We're going to the farm!'

Grandma looked at him with that vacant stare. She held the frame in her lap.

'She's really been quite lost today...' said Amanda in a sad voice.

'No problem. When we get to the farm everything will change.'

So Amanda went to prepare the van. Miguel stayed with Grandma. He thought about all the things they used to do together, going to mass, afternoons on the farm washing his soft toys in the blue bowl, evenings watching *Home Alone* and eating Rich Tea biscuits. This was just another adventure. Perhaps the last. And, who knew, perhaps the best.

Amanda didn't take long. She pushed Grandma in the wheelchair, they went up the ramp into the van and Amanda strapped Grandma into place. Miguel sat next to her. And Amanda, to Miguel's surprise, sat in the driver's seat.

'Are you going to drive?' Miguel asked her.

'Yes, I am! Do you have the address?'

Miguel passed her a scrap of paper with the address and they set off. The journey wasn't long, but Miguel was so nervous and anxious that it felt like they would never arrive. Grandma's hand was clasped tightly in his own. The landscape outside the window was changing from buildings and cars into open plains and trees, farmhouses and animals. Finally, Amanda stopped the car. Through the window, Miguel could see the gate and, a few yards beyond, the house. He became so nervous that he could almost feel the electricity emanating from his fingertips. He felt like shouting and dancing at the same time. But he didn't.

They got out of the car and the first thing to hit them was the smell of the sea, carried on the wings of a gentle breeze. The house that had once been Grandma's was perched almost at the edge of a wide cliff, with a lawn that disappeared from view into an orchard and then a vineyard. The orchard and the vineyard were dancing in the wind, a gentle dance, almost romantic. The house had been repainted and the yellow was no longer the same faded colour as in the photo, but a bright yellow that gleamed in the sun. Ivy had grown up the side of the house. The huge old oak tree, however, was just the same, standing patiently. The leaves fluttering in the wind seemed to be greeting them.

Amanda carefully took Grandma out of the van. Miguel watched her expression, in the hope of seeing her react to the place she had loved so much her whole life. Nothing. Grandma looked around her as if she had never been there, squinting in the sun. But they couldn't turn back now. Miguel walked up fearfully and pressed the button next to the gate. In the distance he could hear the bell ring in the house.

'What a beautiful farm, Miguel. Who lives here now?'

'Some friends of my mum, Alice and Mario.'

And it was at that moment that it dawned on Miguel that he hadn't spoken to the owners of the house about their visit. What if they weren't at home? His heart tight, Miguel rang the bell again. Nothing.

'How strange...' said Amanda. 'Your mum must have told them we were coming, mustn't she? I wouldn't want your grandma to be out here in the sun for long. It's hot.'

Miguel didn't know what to say. He pressed the button again and listened to the distant sound of the bell ringing inside the house. A dog was barking. But no sign of people. Miguel felt an enormous knot form in his throat. After all his effort, the lies, the inventions, even illegalities, after all that it had been in vain. There they were, the three of them, Miguel with a growing sense of guilt, Amanda about to discover the truth and take them home, and Grandma, who would never again enter the house she had dreamed of so often. A flush rose up his neck, staining his face and ears a deep red.

'Miguel?' Amanda called. She spoke in a strange voice that Miguel had never heard. 'Miguel, do you have something to tell me?'

Miguel was about to turn around and admit to everything he had done when he heard the sound of an engine and tyres on the beaten ground. He looked in both directions along the dusty road and then he saw it. A car. Inside were two silhouettes, a man and a woman. Mario and Alice. Relief flooded through him with such force that his knees almost buckled.

He ran to the car as soon as he saw it slow down. Another little lie wouldn't hurt, would it? Now they were so close... Miguel greeted Mario and Alice and explained Grandma's situation. He just made up the fact that his mum had forgotten to ask their permission for the visit. Mario and Alice were a friendly, pleasant couple. Although they were the same age as Miguel's mum, they seemed younger, suntanned, shoulders relaxed, their smiles free and open, as if the air on the farm preserved them in a state of adolescence. They greeted Grandma, who was still apathetic, and Amanda, and told them that yes, of course, they were more than welcome.

It felt like a miracle to be passing through the gate, Alice and Mario in front, Amanda pushing Grandma's wheelchair, and Miguel bringing up the rear. The farm was full of the sound of birds twittering, hopping from tree to tree, and the buzzing of bees in the flowering shrubs. In the background, Miguel could hear the waves beating against the rocks. It was like going back to childhood. He stopped and closed his eyes for a second, letting the sun embrace him. He felt at home.

'Miguel!' called Amanda, from the patio. 'Are you coming?'

Miguel ran through the grass to the patio he knew so well. In it were a watering can and two pairs of wellies.

'Come in, please!' said Alice, seeing Miguel hesitate. 'The dog's in the kitchen, don't worry.'

One on each side, Miguel and Amanda picked up Grandma's wheelchair and climbed the three steps to the entrance and went through the door. Inside was the house of someone who wasn't them. It had a modern look, with pale wood and walls in pastel shades, colourful paintings and photographs of faces he didn't know. Miguel had known the house would be different, decorated in a way he had never seen. But even so, he was shocked when he entered the living room. He bent down to Grandma's level.

'Do you remember this house, Grandma? The house in the photo! I know it isn't the way it was before, but...'

Grandma looked at him, saying nothing. She didn't remember. Nothing had come back to her. Miguel pushed Grandma to the living room window, which looked onto the back garden. It was full of flowers and young trees. Only one thing remained the same: the swing. Grandma looked at the garden and her eyes fixed on that swing. The breeze was becoming stronger and it moved, slowly, backwards and forwards. A slight creaking sound reached them, a sound that Miguel had known his whole life: the swing hooks.

And in his grandmother's brain, something unexpected happened. When she heard the swing, an image appeared in her mind of when she was young, still a child. She recalled how she used to sit on the swing, thrusting with her legs, and doing it quicker and quicker, more forcefully each time, going so high that she thought she would touch the sky. And at that moment, her mother would stick her head out of the living room window and shout:

'Don't swing too high or you'll fall and hurt yourself! Come and have tea!'

And then she would let go of the swing, flying through the air for a few seconds before landing on her feet and hands, like a cat, in the soft grass. In the kitchen her mother would make her toast with butter and honey, sweet and crunchy, the smell of warm bread wafting up her nose and warming her soul. She used to eat it at the kitchen table, with chocolate milk.

She recalled her childhood in that house, how her mother and grandmother knitted, sewed and embroidered. How they made dresses, for her and for her dolls, sometimes to match. She recalled the countless evenings she spent as a teenager, sitting with them on the sofa learning how to do it herself, the radio on and her hands working tirelessly on a new dress.

She remembered getting married. For the first time in years, she could clearly remember her husband, his hunting trips, the dogs, the partridges, the sound of gunshots. She remembered the dog that fell ill, the cough it had, the way it sounded like it was talking. The blue eyes of that man who was boyfriend, then husband, then father and later on grandfather. The man to whom she had devoted a whole life and whom she had forgotten when the illness reached her brain.

She remembered her daughter, Ana. How she had caught her, more than once, spoon in hand giving yoghurt to the dogs. How the little girl's love for animals was so great that she would sleep in the dogs' bed, snuggled up with them. The annual harvests, when Ana wanted to help, but only got in the way, cutting leaves instead of bunches of grapes and leaving behind her a small trail of destruction.

She remembered Miguel, when he was born, the first time he appeared at the farm, in Ana's arms. Seeing him grow, the way he adored milk caramel and jam, the way he would eat quickly to get his pudding sooner. They spent afternoons playing cards, grandmother and grandson, and she let Miguel win, to make him happy. She strolled with her husband and grandson through the orchard, explaining to him the ways of cultivation, admiring the colours and smells of the fruit. She remembered when they cracked walnuts and hazelnuts, what hard work it was, but with the compensation of their joint effort when a warm cake came out of the oven. Other times she left Miguel in the living room watching cartoons and, in the kitchen, she would prepare the 'special dough', which was actually just bread dough. She would put Miguel in an apron and stay there to watch him play, making dolls out of the dough, making up stories with them. When she saw him playing, she felt something inside her melt, her heart full of love for this small boy.

Grandma looked away from the swing that had returned her memories to her and stared at Miguel, now a tall, strong boy, a teenager already. She could remember it all.

'You came back,' said Miguel. It was the only thing he was able to say before falling into a tight embrace.

'My beautiful boy...'

When they moved apart, Miguel watched his grandmother avidly, as if anxious to learn by heart every wrinkle on that happy face he hadn't seen smile openly for so long. In a corner of the room, Amanda, Alice and Mario, watched in silence. Plump tears of genuine emotion were running down Amanda's face.

'Will you take me outside, Miguel?' Grandma asked.

Miguel took Grandma into the garden, pushing the chair. She asked to look at the sea and he agreed. He put her chair in the corner of the garden, between the sea and the house. Grandma watched the sea, sparkling as though it were made of diamonds. And then she gazed at the house, which, to her, was worth more than all the diamonds in the world. Her life had come back to her, the life she had lived, the memories she had made, the world outside of her. She filled her lungs with that air, so full of the past, full of salt and warmth, full of the love of Miguel, who had gone to such effort to bring her here. Full of her love for everything around her, above all her grandson.

'Thank you, thank you, thank you...' she whispered quietly, aware that Miguel could hear her.

Now she could indeed die happy.

ABOUT THIS STORY

'A Frameful of Memories' is a collective work, produced and illustrated by a group of pupils from **Emídio Navarro Secondary School** (Almada, Portugal), under the guidance of writer **Constança Freire de Sousa** between November 2018 and January 2019.

Participating pupils: **Carolina Baptista, Daniela Ribeiro, Deniz Borges, Inês Bernardo, Joana Amaral, Mariana Viana, Pedro Silva, Sofia Sousa** and **Tainá Gurgel.**

ABOUT THE WRITER

Constança Freire de Sousa was born in Porto in 1994. She graduated in 2015 in Media and Communication, specialising in Creative Writing, from Goldsmiths University of London. The following year, she completed a masters in Children's Literature, again with a specialisation in Creative Writing, also from Goldsmiths University of London.

Since then, she has taken part in various creative writing workshops with children and teenagers, both in London and in Portugal. Recently she has been working on a museum project at the University of Porto and the READ ON project, as well as writing articles for the feminist platform *Capazes.*

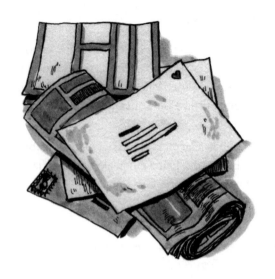

Letters to me

Rita Vilela, in collaboration with students from Fernão Mendes Pinto Secondary School

Translated from Portuguese by Beth Fowler

The moment I opened the door, I saw on the floor an envelope in my favourite colour, with a small heart painted in white instead of a stamp.

Who would go to the trouble of writing me a letter, on paper? And, what's more, come to my house to slip it under the door?

I picked up the envelope, inspecting it closely. Who could it be from? From someone close to me, I was sure, as they knew my favourite colour. From someone who liked me, probably, as they had gone to the trouble of painting the white heart.

I closed my eyes, imagining some of the people who might have written me a love letter... and those I wanted to have written it.

Could it have been Georgie? That cute Australian guy who was in Portugal on an exchange programme? Or Damien O'Brien, who came from Canada and, despite having a Portuguese grandfather, barely spoke the language. Either one of them was capable of choosing to declare themselves in writing, with the help of Google Translate.

But it could just as easily have been Isaac, the Indian boy who was always looking at me, although I had never encouraged him, quite the opposite in fact.

It was odd that the first people I thought of were foreigners. But I managed to come up with some Portuguese possibilities too... Gustavo, for example, my classmate who worked in the pizzeria. I had known for some time that he was into me... Shame it was only weirdos who showed any interest!

Mind you, maybe the letter was from Lourenço. To me, he was by far the most attractive option, with a muscular body (which I had seen, shirtless, running on the beach with his dog).

And there was also the chance that the letter wasn't from a boy. Madalena popped into my head, with her purple hair and alternative look. Yes, it could just as easily have been from her.

And what if this were nothing more than a joke? My brother Duarte, that pest, loved winding me up and was perfectly capable of writing a declaration of love just to mock me.

And just like that, all of a sudden, I couldn't think of anyone else... except for Valentina.

I shook my head to get rid of my thoughts and went back to focusing on the envelope, starting to open it slowly. I stopped halfway, torn between the urge to reveal the mystery and the desire to prolong it. For as long as I didn't see the contents of the letter, I could imagine all the scenarios I liked. For as long as I didn't know what message was contained in that envelope... anything was possible!

I decided to put it off: I dropped the letter, picked up a notebook and pen and wrote the names I had come up with:

Georgie – the Aussie
Damien O'Brien – the Canadian who plays the guitar
Isaac – the Indian boy
Lourenço – the most attractive
Gustavo – the class nerd
Madalena – the alternative girl
Duarte – my irritating brother

I hesitated to add the last name: 'Valentina'. But, even though I was aware that it made no sense, I wrote it down anyway.

I picked up the envelope again, turning it round in my fingers. I held it up to the light from the window, straining to see something. And I did! The words of a carefully written message began to form in front of my eyes.

Love is vague, it can have a thousand definitions, and sometimes I think that perhaps it can't be defined. It's simply something beautiful that, from the day we are born, waits inside us for its moment to be awakened. People can deceive themselves when they believe they 'love' someone, but that will never be the case when it comes to you. You know that old thing about children and teenagers not understanding love? Forget it, it makes no sense!

I didn't like the way this letter was going. I edited the text, adding a bit more emotion.

That's why I, Georgie, am opening my heart to you in the hope that you will let me in. I promise to treat you like the queen of the world.

Yes, that was better! The truth was that I wouldn't have minded if the letter was from Georgie, he was soooo cute!

The words disappeared again and a new letter emerged in my head.

Your fire-coloured hair sets off sparks in my heart. When your emerald eyes meet mine, I feel a crossfire beginning between us. I'm too shy to tell you how precious you are to me. All I can do is open my heart and put down everything I feel on this scrap of paper. I'm ready to love you and support you, always.
With all my love,
Damien

Damien O'Brien had just started at my school. With his slightly dishevelled appearance he seemed something of a bad boy, but his gentle manner indicated the opposite. Most of the girls in the class were unable to resist his charms and were always talking about his blue eyes, his bewitching smile, and that time he played a romantic song on the guitar.

But I would have preferred the author of the letter to be someone else. As friendly, kind and attractive as Damien was, I didn't see him that way.

The words of the letter jumbled up to form a new text.

Dear Helena, my darling Helena...
Since the first time I saw you at the end of the
corridor, I have known that you are the one I want.
Hearing your gentle voice made me realise that
it's you I need. You are the 'x' in my equation,
the piri on my chicken.
Whenever I look at you, I am completely
overwhelmed.
Your Isaac

I could even see the Indian kid slipping the envelope under my door and taking off at a run, filled with shame. Going out with him would have been a nightmare, I was looking for a Prince Charming, not a pest! The last thing I wanted was for it to be Isaac!

A new message appeared, replacing the previous one, which had now vanished.

Helena,
This might seem strange, or even unexpected,
but I feel I have to write you this letter.
I just wanted to tell you that, even though we don't
speak much, I really admire you! Perhaps you think
I'm just another weirdo, but I really like you.
You're so pretty, so friendly, so smiley, so... If I said
everything I feel, I'd never get out of here!
Gustavo

I was keeping my fingers crossed that my admirer wasn't Gustavo. I had no interest in being known as 'the class nerd's girlfriend'. And I didn't need a letter to know that he liked me, I could see it, in Biology class, the way he would throw his pen in my direction, just to give him an excuse to strike up a conversation. And what about the way he blushed when he spoke to me?

Next, Madalena's letter appeared before me.

Helena, Helena, Helena
I know we aren't the same and I'm not the kind of
person you hang out with, but even so I can't stop
thinking about you, and that irritates me. When I see
you, my bleak, depressing world lights up. I dream of
smashing the ice palace around you and getting to
know the real Helena hiding inside. I don't expect you
to return the affection I feel for you. I'm used to it!
But I wanted you to know that it would be a pleasure
to get to know you better.
I don't expect it, but I would like it if you replied.
Madalena

It's strange: although I wasn't properly attracted to Madalena, part of me couldn't help but feel curious and interested in that enigmatic girl. I didn't really understand my feelings, but it flattered me to know that she liked me. I remembered the moment I found out, I was in the toilets at school and my classmates, as always, had found a pretext to humiliate me. Suddenly, Madalena came out of one of the cubicles, put her hand on my shoulder and, her intense eyes boring into mine, said: 'You know you deserve much more than this, don't you?' Ignoring the irate reaction of the girls who were attacking me, she threw me a smile and a wink, before walking away.

But, as I said, the person I wanted it to be was Lourenço. Ever since that day when we shared a desk in Portuguese class, when I started to think he might be 'the one'. As well as friendly and romantic, he was the most attractive boy at school, he had all the requirements and characteristics I always looked for... Having him would be a dream come true!

I didn't even need him to write very much, just the essentials:

My dear Helena,
I want you to remember this letter forever,
as the moment when I opened my heart to you.
The truth is that I'm completely in love with you
and want to live a beautiful love story with you.
A kiss, with much love,
Lourenço

Unfortunately, in this case, I suspected I was going to be left with my 'dreams', I didn't think for a minute that the letter was from Lourenço. In reality, the most likely scenario was that it was my brother Duarte. I had never known him to miss an opportunity to mess with me. And, for someone who had cut my blouses into pieces and tried to cover me with paint on the way to school... this would be nothing! But, if it was that little brat, he knew very well what the response would be. I was no fool, I knew how to tell if the letter was false.

I feel like we are destined for each other and I know that the sooner I admit it to you, the sooner I'll be able to relieve this burning sensation in my chest. Whenever I see you at school, I feel like my heart's going to explode, I can't help losing myself in your sweet green eyes and I imagine myself sailing the scarlet waves of your hair.
When we can't be together, the distance that separates us consumes me, it empties my lungs of air...

Yes, 'burning in my chest,' 'heart's going to explode,' 'sailing on scarlet waves', that was Duarte's style... that and the spelling mistakes, but I didn't include those in my mind's eye, they looked too messy.

Please don't let the envelope be from him! Let it not be from him! I begged. Discovering that the message had been written by my brother would have been the worst outcome of the mystery. The letter was too pretty, it would have been a waste!

And what if it was from Valentina? I should explain that Valentina was someone who was fundamentally different from me. Where I hesitated... she was decisive. Where I was trapped by other people's opinions... she moved forward, sure of her options. I saw the glass half empty... she saw it half full. Where I failed... she achieved. We couldn't have been more different!

I imagined a message from her:

Helena Valentim
Tell me who you are
Not how people see you
Or who you long for

In the eyes of the world
Your life is ideal
When the truth is
It's such an ordeal

Admired by many
But loved? By no one
In the lonely night-time
It's just you, all alone

The time has now come
To change everything
But change for yourself
Let love sing!

Despite the differences, Valentina was the only person

who worried about me, who cared what I thought and felt, who knew me and understood me... The only one!

She was the only one I had ever opened up to and who knew that I had been feeling bad since, after an argument about me, my parents decided to separate. To make things worse, my classmates found out and thought that the divorce was a good subject to mock. And the tragic incident with my cousin was the final blow, but I didn't even want to think about that.

Until now, I had been putting off solving the mystery, preferring my imagination to reality. But, what if reality brought me true love? With that idea in my head, I opened the envelope.

What was this? An advert for Valentine's Day?! My beautiful love letter had turned out to be an advert?! I felt like swearing.

Furious, I grabbed that piece of rubbish and tossed it in the bin. But, just as it left my hands, I noticed a word that seemed to be underlined at the bottom. I picked it up again, inspecting the text more carefully. There were in fact several syllables and letters that were underlined. I grabbed my pen and wrote down everything that seemed to be highlighted, grouping the letters into words, until I got something coherent:

'Follow the clues, rise to the challenges and you will find love!' The rest of the phrase was rather cryptic: 'Seek pink maiden and modest guardians of magic manuscripts'. I smiled, I liked mysteries.

My eyes flitted between the building opposite and the small piece of paper I held in my hands. I was on a Lisbon street that was painted pink and, opposite, was a café with the sign 'Maiden and Modest,' the walls of which were covered with books, shelves and shelves full of books. The ceiling had paintings the like of which I had never seen. The only reason for my presence there the enigma I was trying to decipher.

I went in and looked for the book *The Guardians of the Magic Manuscripts*, the name of which was in the message, I found it and opened it. Inside was a small piece of card with an instruction on it: 'Tell us your greatest strengths and confess your greatest desire.' I went along with it, deciding to be honest, I asked to borrow a pen and I wrote: 'I'm creative, good at drawing and dreaming. I want to have true friends.' Then I put the card back inside the book and returned home, believing that the third message would appear there... But it didn't! It arrived via email, from an unknown address.

The days that followed were quite an adventure, searching for clues and challenges that appeared in the strangest places. To give just a few examples: a message was delivered to me by a stranger who approached me in a café; I found another in the pocket of my waterproof jacket; when I went into the classroom, after break time, there was an envelope on my desk. And that wasn't the only mystery I found at school, there was also a tiny text written on the toilet door (whoever wrote it knew me well, they even knew which cubicle I tend to use!).

But now, at 5.30pm on a sunny Sunday, that mysterious journey was approaching its end. If I was right, on the second floor of that building I would find the final challenge... or the well-deserved prize. If my expectations were answered, at the top of the stairs I could see through the window, I would meet my love, my true love.

I looked at my watch again, there were still 29 minutes to go. I used those spare minutes to think back on some of the challenges I had had to overcome to get here. This treasure hunt that someone had created just for me had led me to do things of which I had never thought myself capable.

'Fight your fears.' The first challenge was written on the ticket for a beginner's climbing session. And so, at nine o'clock on a Saturday morning, there I was, dangling from ropes, scaling the steep climbing wall, while mentally I was fighting one of my biggest demons: a fear of heights. With the instructor's encouragement, and after a great deal of halting and hesitation, I managed to reach the top of the wall. Then came the most difficult part: trusting, gathering the courage to let go of the holds and allow myself to come down. When I placed my feet back on the floor, I remember having thought: 'If I can do this, I can do anything!' I didn't know that, despite the fear it had caused me, that was one of the 'easy' tests.

'Increase your strength' was the message that came with a voucher for a series of karate classes. Let's go, I thought, although I wasn't at all suited to the sport, I didn't really like being touched, and I thought fighting was dangerous. At the end of the ten classes, I could hardly believe it... despite the pain of the experience, I left the karate centre with a smile on my face, relaxed, satisfied with my progress, and feeling much more confident. And the strangest thing was that, when I imagined the spiteful girls in my class mocking me, I wasn't scared and felt able to say to them: 'That's enough!'

The next message sent me to the city's chess park, where I found a padlocked box and a mathematical formula that would give me the code to open it. But, although we had covered that kind of formula in Maths, I didn't know what to do with it. I looked around me and saw, sitting on a bench with a book, my classmate Gustavo, the class nerd. He would certainly be able to find the solution to the problem, but I would have to ask him. And, after a bad experience, I had promised myself that I would never again ask for help from anyone at that school. I hated asking for help!

But either I spoke to him or ran the risk of being eliminated from the treasure hunt, and so I went up to him. I was surprised with the result: Gustavo was really friendly and, with a practical example, he helped me understand something that had seemed extremely complicated in class.

I solved the equation, opened the box and found a new message. Perhaps asking for help every now and then wasn't so bad!

'Don't put off a difficult conversation' was written in the next message. What difficult conversations did I need to

196

have? My brain immediately began to search and I soon thought of one: speaking to my parents about the divorce. Until that day, I had been alternating between 'feeling I was to blame for the separation' and 'blaming my parents for separating without thinking of me'. The time had come to talk to them about it. I took advantage of my dad visiting the house and them both being there, and I forced myself to do it. I never thought it would be so hard to take the first step... but it paid off! It was a serious, mature conversation, and it made me realise that I wasn't responsible for the divorce and that they had the right to decide how they wanted to live their lives. And I was also sure that, together or separated, my parents would still love me, always, unconditionally!

The final challenge was open to interpretation: 'Choose a situation in which the past has tormented you and face up to it.' As soon as I read the message, my cousin's face appeared before my eyes. Ever since I had learnt of his death, in a terrible fire, I had only wanted to forget what had happened. I had invented an excuse not to go to his funeral and, with that weighing on my conscience, I felt the guilt of not being there that day. If this was the final challenge, I had no option but to overcome it, but my success in the previous tests helped me gather the strength to visit my cousin in his final resting place.

Visiting that graveyard was, out of everything I had ever done in life, the thing that I found hardest. As soon as I entered the cemetery, I started to cry, convulsive tears that wouldn't stop... But I didn't give up, I went up to the gravestone with his name on it and told him everything I had kept inside me that I had wanted to say to him since his death. Instead of feeling sad, I went home relieved.

Alternating with the challenges, there was another remarkable component to this treasure hunt: the requests for friendship. I received eight, each one signed with different capital letter. All of them began with a personal introduction and finished with the phrase: *'I want to be your friend, a true friend. Will you accept my friendship?'* I had responded to all of them with a resounding 'yes'. If the requests were genuine, I wanted to have people like that in my life.

I took advantage of the time I had to wait and started to re-read the introductions that had come with the various requests, pausing at the parts that had made the biggest impression on me.

The introduction from 'M' came first: *My mum died when I was 8, my dad started to drink around then, and I felt more alone than ever. And only now, ten years later, has he finally got help, he joined Alcoholics Anonymous, and he's starting to show signs of improvement.* The text continued, but that was the most significant part.

Someone who signed with the letter 'I' had written: *My parents came to Portugal looking for a better life. It isn't easy to provide for seven children! Sometimes there was nothing to eat in the house, clothes were passed down from the oldest to the youngest... I was used to it. But the only thing I never got used to was hearing, in words or gestures: 'go back to your own country.' When I do, I can't help feeling a knot in my throat.*

From the next request, belonging to a 'G', I chose an excerpt: *Sometimes I dream of a world where we don't need to be the same as each other to be accepted.*

Those messages told me that I wasn't the only one to have problems. After a bit of reflection, I was left with the idea that, at least on occasion, I might have contributed to increasing other people's problems. I felt ashamed.

Then I moved onto the message from a 'JB': *I was born in a small town. It was very poor, but the people there, despite their difficulties, instead of complaining, looked for solutions to the problems that came up... I'm grateful for having been taught that, regardless of what life throws at us, the way we react to it is our own choice.*

The introduction from 'DO' had many things in it, but there was one phrase that was most revealing: *'I think everyone should have a hobby. Mine is music... it's the best way for me to communicate... it's an escape from all of my problems.'*

The alarm on my wrist vibrated, interrupting my reading and telling me that the twenty-nine minutes had passed. The time had come!

I rang the bell, I saw the light on the security camera come on and I heard the latch opening, without anyone trying to communicate through the intercom.

I climbed the stairs and, heart pounding, waited for door 2B to open, without the faintest idea what was going to happen.

'Surprise!' In front of me was Josh Barley, who was the most positive person I knew, and the closest thing I had to a friend. Behind Josh were my brother, Georgie, Damien, Isaac, Lourenço and even Madalena. 'Surprise!' they shouted again, in chorus, seeming to expect me to react.

But how could I react, when I didn't have a clue what was going on?

Josh Barley explained that it was he who had brought the group together, because he saw that I wasn't right, that I was hitting rock bottom. And, all together, they had devised those challenges and they had declared their friendship, signing with their initials.

That revelation meant a lot. What they had done to help me showed that they liked me, that I was important to them, that they truly were my friends.

But there was something that still didn't make sense: why that specific group of people? It couldn't be a coincidence!

'It was me,' Duarte confessed. 'After your first reply, Josh spoke to me, he wanted to know who we could get involved in 'Operation Helena', and I went into your room and found an open notebook with a list of names... The only one we couldn't find was Valentina. Who is she?

I shrugged my shoulders without replying. I couldn't reveal that Valentina is a part of me, my best part, incidentally. When she started to lose the strength to assert herself, I started to imagine that she had abandoned me and become a real person. If my brother knew that Valentina was... well... a kind of imaginary friend, he'd think I was crazy.

I looked around me: in that room were all my friends, only Valentina was missing.

And then I realised that she was there too, not next to them, but inside me, where she belonged.

The group had done what it had promised: I, Helena Valentim, had ended up finding love: the love of friends, the love of family... and love for myself!

ABOUT THIS STORY

'Letters to me' is a collective work, produced and illustrated by a group of pupils from different school years in **Fernão Mendes Pinto Secondary School** (Almada, Portugal), under the guidance of writer **Rita Vilela** and with the support of teacher **Lurdes Ferreira** between November 2018 and January 2019.

Participating pupils: **Ana Ressurreição, Beatriz Fernandes, Francisco Ressurreição, Hugo Rolo, João Góis, Julieta S. Goncalves, Madalena Pulquério, Marta Vicente, Pedro Tavares** and **Raquel Silva**.

ABOUT THE WRITER

Rita Vilela was born in 1964 and her first book was published in 2008. After she graduated in Psychology, she pursued a career in education, combining this work with providing therapy, writing and other activities linked to words – and people.

Her bibliography includes the historical fantasy saga *The Descendants of Merlin,* the fantasy and adventure trilogy *The 7 Colours of Oníris,* and the children's collection *Alice*, among many others. Her aims of promoting a joy of reading, facilitating learning and planting seeds of change are clearly visible in her writing. In 2013 she branched out across borders and now has 10 books available internationally, distributed in Brazil, Italy and Venezuela. In 2018, her books had sold over 200,000 copies.

The words that live within us

Susana Amorim, in collaboration with students from Romeu Correia Secondary School

Translated from Portuguese by Beth Fowler

(DAY OF BIRTH)

When André was born, he heard his first sound.

In truth, he had heard some sounds while he was still in the safety of his mother's belly – a calm symphony that made him feel cherished and protected.

But this was a different sound. Stronger and more penetrating, with a variety of tones and rhythms he didn't recognise.

The moment he heard it, and was enveloped by that intense light, he was frightened, realising that a world of noise was awaiting him. And he cried. He cried so much that yet another sound invaded him – his own sound.

Even so, something told him that this was an amazing world too!

(AS A BABY)

From a very early age, any words he heard he loved. And André would smile.

His mother's and father's voices were the sounds he liked best. They gave him protective and comforting words:
'I'm here, you're beautiful, my love, food, happy'

There were also bright, smiling words:
'Play, granny, grandpa, songs, walk, look'

And relaxing words:
'Bath, sleep, nappy, lap, cuddles'

(FROM THE AGE OF EIGHTEEN MONTHS, NOW WALKING)

Little by little, André realised that he too had things to say and he started to try to form words. The fascinating sound that each one produced between his lips encouraged him to start talking very early.

Hi was his first word; a seed of a word that grew into others.

Then, he discovered *No* – a strong word, which he used a lot as he grew. He realised, early on, the importance of this word, as it always caused a reaction and he was often able to state his intention with it.

(SLIGHTLY OLDER – 3-4 YEARS OLD)

For André, words had a texture and he liked to touch them. They also had a smell and taste and he loved to feel them. Each one had its own musicality, which is why he began to choose them with care.

He liked playful words:

'Park, friends, ball, laugh, run, water, toys, merry-go-round'

And he loved curious words:
'Bugs, search, discover, soil, test'

And sometimes, just sometimes, he could choose sweet words, that melted in his mouth:
'Cotton candy, ice cream, chocolate, popcorn'

(PRIMARY SCHOOL – 6-7 YEARS OLD)

André was becoming richer and richer in words. He treated them with affection and chose the nicest ones to give generously to others.

'Do you want to play with me?'

The truth was that the more words he discovered, the easier he found it to say what he wanted.

'Good morning, Miss' was now the melody that accompanied him every day.

At school, he enunciated each new word with great care.
'Sit down, pen-cil, rub-ber, lett-ers, num-bers, ex-er-ci-ses'

205

There were some he really liked.
'*Playtime, friends, football, laugh, talk out loud, run*'

Others, he didn't like quite so much...
'*Write, neatly, rub it out, do it again*'

In time, the words became tiring and repetitive.
'*Sit down, pen-cil, rub-ber, lett-ers, num-bers, ex-er-ci-ses, write, neatly, rub it out, do it again*'

The truth is that André was accumulating so many words that, at a certain point, silence began to impose itself over the music of the words.

André started to lose some of the words that had been part of him before.
'*Joy, spontaneity, curiosity*'

And, secretly, he looked for some other words that he needed.
'*Support, confidence, imagination, rest, novelty*'

(ADOLESCENCE − 11-14 YEARS OLD)

André grew, and with him grew the mountain of words yet to be said.

The more words he collected, the more they echoed inside him.

He had words caught in his throat.
'*Instability, transformation, acceptance, problems, difference*'

He felt risky words coursing through his body.

'Adventure, desire, experiences, danger, rebellion, impulsiveness, influences'

He was doubled over by painful words.

'Insecurity, uncertainty, isolation, conflict, exclusion, fear, disappointment'

Little by little, the noise of the world mingled with the words that ran confusedly through him.

(**YOUNG MAN – 15 YEARS ONWARDS**)

Until, one day, everything changed. André can remember that moment clearly! The teacher introduced herself and asked them to tell her a bit about themselves. For this, she gave them a large blank sheet of paper, paints and paintbrushes.

André, who had forgotten the words that defined him, such was his confusion, looked inside for a few moments and tried to read himself. First, he found a mess of words with no meaning or connection. Then, he tried to reorder them and even decided to throw some words out. The truth is that the more André moved and sorted all those words hidden in the corners of his body, the more he felt like master of them again.

Little by little, the paintbrush came to life and the words echoed a new symphony...

And André painted visionary words.

'New me, start, future, discovery, development, feelings, world'

He brought essential words to life.

'Friendship, family, goals, responsibility, perseverance'

And, finally, he finished his work with the most precious word he had discovered inside himself; a colourful word, soft, comforting and bright.

'Love'

(END)

André never again felt those grey words inhabit him for too long.

There were others that he made a point of colouring in, so that they could grow and fill out inside him.

One thing is for certain, and that is that he never again stopped painting them, and he felt proud to show them and share them.

At the end of the year, encouraged by their teacher, André and his classmates organised an activity for the whole school, which was very special for everyone. It was called:

'What are the words that live inside you?'

Some people sang their words in songs, others expressed them in drawing, painting, writing, with gestures, dances, disguises...

ABOUT THIS STORY

'The words that live within us' is a collective work, produced and illustrated by a Year 12 class from **Romeu Correia Secondary School** (Feijó, Portugal) between November 2018 and March 2019 under the guidance of writer **Susana Amorim**, coordinated by teacher **Ana Prates**, with the collaboration of **Samuel Figueiredo** and the support of teacher librarians **Isabel Pinheiro** and **Natália Pinto**.

Participating pupils: **Ana Rita Barreta, Ana Rodrigues, Andreia Costa, Beatriz Bispo, Beatriz Rocha, Catarina Tavares, Cristiana Costa, David Seita, Diogo Cidades, Diogo Gonçalves, Eduardo Fonseca, Inês Condinho, Ísis Gregório, Márcia Mendonça, Mariana Ferreira, Mariana Fonseca, Melissa Carrão, Sara Barata, Tatiana Neto** and **Vanessa Coelho**.

ABOUT THE WRITER

Susana Amorim was born in 1976 in the district of Aveiro, and she graduated in Psychology in 2001. Her career has focused primarily on children and young people, in both preventive and therapeutic contexts. She is currently at the 'Emotions Office' – Clínica Goarman Pessoa – where she works in Emotional Health, providing individual and family counselling. She promotes school sessions through her books and emotional skills programmes, which she writes herself.

Her first books were published in 2014, based on her experience as a psychotherapist, with the aim of providing support tools for families, experts and teachers, offering a playful, informal approach to various themes relating to children.

Three Steps to Learn How to Fly

André Fernandes, in collaboration with students from Cacilhas Secondary School

Translated from Portuguese by Beth Fowler

The first time I died was when I heard the sound of the engine stealing my father from me. From us. In my mother's eyes, I could sense the pain of what had been taken away from us. This was all long before you came into my life and yet, now I come to think of it, with all that you came to teach me, you were already there.

That engine burnt up the resolve of the men speeding off towards a war they hadn't chosen, one that had chosen them, on the noble mission of halting the evil that had insinuated itself in the world. Nothing had been learnt with the first war, so a second was needed to confirm that there is only one way to live on this planet. But living in peace doesn't suit all men. It didn't suit those who took my father from us. He left with a promise to return, but that was a promise yet to be fulfilled. I could see my pain mirrored in my mother's eyes. A child of my age didn't understand the war and, to me, going to Normandy was no different to going from our house to the park, or to the market. I remember seeing a look of petrification on her pale face, which, now that I'm older, I recognise as an absurd fear of dying alone, a chill in her guts that few would understand. On that first day, my mother's lacklustre gaze hid the fragility of her tightening heart and, without my realising, at that precise moment, my heart, too, started to close in on itself. My father was the pragmatic one, the voice of reason. My mother, the emotional one, was the core of affection. Together, they were the roots that nourished the fruit that I could have been, had those roots not been severed by the war, as though love were a weed. When that engine burst into life, dry and incredibly noisy, and I saw my father's proud head disappear between the hills on the horizon and heard my mother's contained weeping, I felt that a part of me had been extinguished, leaving me with just a misshapen lump of fear and guilt, like when the lamp was switched off in my room at night, after a goodnight kiss from my parents. Then the monsters might come and devour me.

That day, my mother started to become someone she was not. She hid her emotions, to protect me from mine. That day became the routine and, as time progressed, she became increasingly distant. Her touch was no longer a caress. Her lips were no longer kisses. Her breath ceased to be life. While initially it hurt to see the table set for three with my father's place ready, but empty, on the days that followed it hurt more to see nothing there. My mother stopped living before my father had died. Losing him meant losing herself, and losing them meant losing myself. For weeks, at a tender age when, without blossoming, I matured beyond my years, it was I who set the table for three and ate alone.

I waited for my mother to come downstairs, for my father to return and for food to once again slip down my throat with the pleasure with which I had once savoured it. But my mother didn't come downstairs and my father could no longer choose to return. 'Mummy, when is Daddy coming back?' I asked her every night when I went to give her the kiss that she used to give me. She never replied. One day, she dragged out the words I'll never forget: 'Your father won't be coming back.' I continued to set the table for three. I didn't cry for days. Months, perhaps: time ceases to exist when you're in pain. Until I heard the news on the radio. The Allies had won. All this sacrifice had not been in vain. I cried. I cried a lot. 'He won. He's going to come back!' But the days passed and the only thing to return was my mother's phrase, which dragged itself into my soul.

'Your father won't be coming back.' I continued setting the table for three. It was when, during one of my solitary dinners, I heard the post-war news on the radio, all about the returns, the rehabilitation of a destroyed Europe, that I began to cry for the defeat that that victory meant for me: I had lost my parents. I lost them in the name of a sacrifice I hadn't chosen to make. Why me? I threw the dishes on the floor. Why us? I broke the radio. My mother didn't come downstairs to see what was happening. And I stopped groping blindly for a love that wasn't coming. I was alone. I felt alone. And that was how it would be, from that day. Never again would I allow love to make me suffer. If love was suffering, I was determined not to suffer anymore.

The second time I died might not have been exactly the second, chronologically speaking, but I remember it as such. When you die several times, like I died during that childhood that was stolen from me, the piece that is taken away from us is never as large as the first one. Gradually, those pieces become smaller and it becomes easier to give them up, because we become less. We are lighter. Less formed. I apologise for rambling through these explanations for my pain, but towards the end of life, we find greater clarity to see what was once dark. Perhaps the end is just the possibility that life will finally give us an understanding of the journey. But you're a good listener, aren't you? You always were. The second time I died, as I was telling you, was in the middle of the journey. I wasn't prepared for that love. But, if I could have been prepared, would it really have been love?

A surgeon: I had sworn to myself that I would live within the cocoon of that mission: saving lives, without having to fight for it. The chill of the losses I had inherited in my youth allowed me to embrace a profession in which loss was a certainty. I prepared many families for the worst and delivered news of success to others. With the former, I could never find the right words. With the latter, I lacked euphoria, never able to overcome the echoing feeling of 'you did nothing more than your obligation.' I spoke to them the way I spoke to my inner child, as though to someone whose losses had come abruptly in life. Losses that had made me feel that, in some way, I should have saved them, as though that were my obligation. We always speak the language we learn, don't we? Perhaps that's what was missing. Learning a new language. Learning a new life. That was when all this began. When I saw her honey-coloured eyes on the operating table, drifting off with the anaesthesia, I felt something I hadn't felt since childhood: comfort. It was the first time I had looked into those eyes and, even so, I seemed to be seeing her for the umpteenth time. Who could this woman be? What history and what stories was she hiding? What was this effect she was having on me? The surgery went well and, when she woke up, it was up to me to break the news of its success. Her serenity melted my coldness. The kindness of her gaze awoke my smile. Could this really be happening? Let me tell you: not only can it happen, but it did happen. And it was one of the most beautiful experiences of my life.

You must be wondering, then, why I died for the second time, isn't that so? Don't be in a hurry to find out the answers. Often they are to be found on the path that leads us to them. As soon as she woke from the operation and saw me, she uttered, with a smile, words that said more than they seemed to: 'Long time no see, doctor.' I didn't know how to react. I hid my desire to smile: that wasn't why I was there. It was in the days that followed, during my – genuine – doctor's rounds, that she started to delve into a part of me that had been dormant since I had learnt that loving is suffering. At one of these visits, as I told her how well her recovery was going, she let her gaze drift out of the window and said to me: 'We take everything for granted, don't you think?' I stayed defensively silent. 'Those trees. Those leaves. That wind blowing through them.' Still silence. 'Life, doctor. We always take life for granted.' I started to get agitated. This generalisation was no use to me.

'Some people take life for granted, others death,' I told her. 'Is that the case with you?'

She looked me in the eye. 'Was that why you chose this profession?' How could someone else's composure seem so challenging?

'You want to know too much!' I told her, with a mixture of politeness and severity.

'I don't know who you lost, doctor. But they're still living out there.' She looked out of the window and my gaze followed hers, pausing for moments that seemed like eternities, watching the delicate leaves fluttering

215

in the breeze. 'It's the wind. No death can stop it.' She smiled. 'When I get out of here, I'm going to get closer to the wind. I like having picnics in nature, so that I never forget that I am nothing more than a gust of wind.' I looked at her with the distrust of someone who wants to know more and the curiosity of someone distrustful of finding out. She noticed my expression and said, with her characteristic smile: 'You should come too, doctor. There's such a pretty spot in the city park. You'd like it.' I said goodbye, but I took those words with me. Secretly, at night, I began to look forward the following day's visit, to listen to more of what she had to say. I couldn't get fond of her, though. A few days later she was going to do what love had always done in my life: leave.

On the day she was discharged, I couldn't look her in the eye. 'So, today is your last day here. I hope I don't see you again!' That was perhaps the only lie I ever told her. From the corner of my eye, I saw her watching me, standing next to the bed, already dressed to leave, still with that kind, serene smile.

'Thank you,' she breezed in her sweet voice. I wasn't used to verbalised thanks. Or, if I did hear them, I wasn't used to listening. But she made sure I did: 'Gratitude, doctor, is what makes the breeze gentle. Even when it comes as a gust. We have to say thank you. Thank you to life... The life we're given to live. That's why I'm thanking you. For what you have done by appearing in mine.'

'I did nothing more than my...'

She interrupted me. 'No, doctor. It isn't your obligation I'm thanking you for: it's having made the choice to be guided by it.' She held out her hand to me. I looked her in the eye and held out mine. When my right palm touched her right palm, our destinies superimposed and the shiver I felt was the first chink in the armour I had closed myself in since I was a boy. When I met her, something told me that it wasn't the first time I had seen her. When I said goodbye, the same inner voice made me believe that it wouldn't be the last time. I wasn't wrong.

The following Saturday, I decided to go to the city park. I don't know whether I was looking for her or looking for myself, but I know that, on that day, I found a bit of both. Of all three of us, because that was where I met you. I took the cloth my mother used to put on the table and the lunchbox my father used to take to work, unused since I had lost them. I spread the cloth out on the grass, set out the quick meal I had prepared and sat down to eat. I saw couples strolling past holding hands, dogs running loose, children taking their first steps.

I looked up to gaze at the sky and saw the leaves of the tree I was leaning against, waving gently in that all-important breeze. I closed my eyes and let the tears flow. Was this gratitude for everything I had been, for everything I was and for everything I would be? When I opened my eyes, there was a smile above me, watching. 'I knew you'd come, doctor.' I didn't reply. I hurriedly dried my tears. I didn't want her to see me like this. 'Why are you drying them?' she asked.

'Are you always like this?' I answered.

'Curious?'

'Impertinent.' She smiled.

'I know that your coldness hides tears, doctor. No one is born cold. And what's more, we can always recognise a look we've seen in our own eyes when we see it in someone else's.'

'Have you already dried your tears?'

'Yes, I have. But I don't do that anymore.' She sat down next to me. 'And why did you cry them?' I asked.

'That's where we are different. You ask me why I cried them, doctor, I ask you why you dried them.' We sat watching the silence those words left hanging in the air.

'Because they remind me of the reason I cried,' I said.

'And what reason is that?'

'Having loved.'

'Perhaps you'll stop drying your tears when you realise that it isn't love that makes you cry them.'

'Perhaps you'll stop thinking you know everything, when you hear everything I have to tell you.'

'What love was it that made you stop loving?'

'The love of my parents, which I no longer have.' I told her about my losses. Without my realising, the armour continued to break into pieces.

'And, now that you've told me, do you still think it's love that makes you cry?'

'If it isn't love, what is it?'

'Loss. That's what hurts.'

'And what do you know about that?'

'The same. My story is yours.' I looked at her in surprise.

'Did you lose your parents too?'

'Yes, to the war.' She told me her story. It was an exact reflection of mine. The empathy of those words started to rebuild the broken bridges that had cut me off from others. For the first time, I cried for the pain of someone who wasn't me and, in that shared pain, I realised that I wasn't alone. My cocoon continued to shatter. When my hand reached up to dry my tears, hers found it. 'Don't dry them. Don't you get it? They are the proof that love existed.' I allowed my hand to be guided by hers. She placed it on the grass. 'Don't blame life. Don't blame your parents. And above all, don't blame yourself.'

'How can I, when it was life that took them away from me, they are the ones who have gone and it was me that it happened to?'

'Because the life that took them away from you was also the life that gave them to you, because they were present to the point where you felt their absence and because this is all part of creating the person you are, precisely because it happened to you.'

'Do you know what it means not to have a mother's touch when life hurts?'

'Your mother was sick. It wasn't your mother who didn't touch you. It was the sickness of loss that took that ability away from her. For many, loss is a sickness.'

'Isn't it just.' I told her how I waited for a love that

never came. I told her about all the times I had set the table for three, with a hope that hurt so much it took everything out of me. I told her how I searched for my mother until I stopped finding her. I cried. Without drying my tears, I cried.

'Loss is the possibility of filling the void with the memory of the love that was or the love we would have liked it to be,' she told me.

Her hand was still resting on mine, in the grass. That's when you appeared. For the first time, you appeared. You perched on our hands and, like someone running into an old friend they haven't seen for a while, she smiled, just as I saw you appear and perch on us with your fragile beauty.

'You know, we're just like her,' she said, with a delicate gesture in your direction, so that you didn't fly away. 'We love in three phases. In the first, we crawl around searching for love and we confuse that love with pain; in the second, we close ourselves in a protective cocoon to ensure that we won't get hurt, because we think we have learnt that love hurts us.' She paused. Your wings fluttered to the rhythm of her words. '

And in the third phase?'

'In the third? In the third, we use the strength of the pain that imprisoned us to break the cocoon, determined to grow wings and, finally, fly towards what love really is: a permanent act of letting go.' I let myself go with the beauty of her words and gave her the first of our many kisses. I felt my soul tearing from my body the pain I had been trapped in all that time, breaking it into shards. Time, in that instant, disappeared. In love, too, time ceases to exist. When I drew back from the kiss that I couldn't draw back from, I looked at our hands on the grass, next to my mother's table cloth and my father's lunch box. You were still there, fluttering along to it all. I smiled. She smiled back and said to me: 'I'm glad you set the table for three again, doctor.'

'Perhaps it's time to address each other a bit more intimately,' I replied, emotionally.

'You're right, my love,' she said. You disappeared and I stopped living in the cocoon I had been enclosed in until then.

The days that followed were a crescendo of discovery in a chapter I had thought I would never experience again. Every day, after work, I had someone with whom to share my adventures and misadventures. I savoured those moments when I had the certainty of sharing. It's funny how that assurance of sharing makes us more present when we are alone. From time to time, she surprised me, turning up at my work without warning, so that we wouldn't miss each other. Sometimes, she brought me a meal she had cooked. Other times, cake and a coffee. Other times, she appeared with nothing, but she knew that she was everything. It was when I began to want to return the favour that I realised she hadn't told me where she lived, nor had she allowed me to find out. Fear began to seize me: what was she hiding? One day when she visited me, not realising that my shift was about to finish, I decided to follow her. My anxiety and guilt at what I did still convince me that it wasn't the best approach, but it was fed by my fear. She caught a taxi and I followed in my car, as if on auto-pilot. My heart accelerated with the car and my stomach was spinning like the wheels. Where was she heading? When the taxi indicated to pull in, I made sure that I stopped a few metres away so that I didn't curtail her movements. I saw her pay the driver and get out. She went towards the hotel outside which the car had stopped. I didn't know what to do. 'A hotel? What is she doing in a hotel?' I sat in the car for a few hours, but ended up driving away without having seen her come out. That night, I couldn't sleep. My childhood abandonment was testing me with the images of fear it produced in me: who could she have been meeting? Why had she never mentioned visits to a hotel? And why was she avoiding telling where I could find her, in case I wanted to visit her? Unspoken doubts become internalised answers and I started to internalise mine, my behaviour towards her becoming distant. I followed her again and she always went there. What was behind this strange habit?

It was in our park that I found the answer.

We had arranged another of our picnics and, despite my fear, I agreed to go. My doubts were still hungry for answers, which prevented me from fleeing completely from the fear she was causing me. When I arrived, she kissed me on the forehead. She looked calm as usual. I didn't, though, and she was always able to tell who I was, above and beyond what I showed myself to be. 'We need to talk about that frown of yours,' she told me. 'What's the matter with you?' Nothing, nothing was the matter. That afternoon was filled with anxious, tense silences. I really wanted to ask her about the hotel, but to do that would be to admit to my clandestine behaviour which, in her eyes, would make me look like a psychopath. After an inner struggle, the desire to ask overcame.

'Where do you go after you've been with me?'

'What?'

'Where do you usually go, after you've been with me?'

'Where do I usually go? Home, of course.' That response hit me right in the stomach and I lost control of my emotions.

'Why are you lying?' Her expression remained serene and that made me even more uncomfortable.

'Lying? What on earth are you saying? What's wrong with you?'

'I think it's time to bring all this to an end,' I told her. I wanted to hurt her before she hurt me.

'Why do I get the feeling that this is your fear speaking and not your love?'

'Perhaps because you know what you've been doing,' I continued evasively.

'Could you please tell me your fears with love?' she asked me. 'I promise I will listen to them with the same love.'

'You don't go home.' This time, it was she who frowned.

223

She shook her head, looking down and, with a slight smile, said:

'Has it never occurred to you that perhaps we call different places home?' I was intrigued. 'Instead of spying on me and torturing yourself with subterfuge and suppositions, why don't you come right out and ask me everything you want to know?' I plucked up the courage I didn't feel and exhaled the question I feared:

'What do you do in the hotel where I've seen you so many times?'

'I live there.'

'You live in a hotel?'

'Not really. It's temporary.' A pause followed. 'The only reason I'm not really angry with you is because this is all part of something I've been hiding from you,' she told me. My anxiety intensified. Realising this, she soothed me. 'Calm down. Don't think that I've been disrespectful. I would never do that.'

'So what on earth are you hiding from me? Tell me right now!'

'I didn't tell you because I didn't even know how to express it all. When I met you, I had just sold my house because I accepted a job offer abroad. It's my dream job, I've waited a lifetime for this opportunity and I really want to go and fulfil what I feel is my mission in the world. But I didn't want to lose you. When you appeared, I delayed my departure. I used some of the money from the house sale to live in that hotel. That's why you see me go back there every day and that's why I never told you where I live, nor did I encourage you to visit me or surprise me. I love you, but I know I'm going to lose you and I've been putting off facing that reality, because I don't want to suffer and, above all, I don't want to see you suffer.'

The jumble of emotions overwhelming me was hard to put into words. Torn between sadness, disgust and rage, I followed my impulse to get up and leave. What I had feared when I met her had been confirmed: we had reached the point where it was safer for me to leave than to watch someone I loved leave me again. The second time I died, as I told you, was right there, in the middle of the journey. Life couldn't be repeating itself. It couldn't! It just wasn't possible for that love to be taken away from me like this. How many more times did I have to lose a great love to convince me that love made me suffer? I started to walk in no particular direction. She stayed sitting and didn't follow me. The engine of my stride was as noisy as the one that had stolen away my father. The paleness of my frightened face was the same as the paleness that had stolen my mother's. When I came to my senses, I was on the other side of the park. I lay down next to a tree and cried out all that whirlwind of emotions. I was angry. Angry that she had hidden it from me, angry at the truth she had now told me. Angry. Very angry. I punched the grass a few times and you took flight. I hadn't even noticed that you were there, resting, contemplating my agitation. Through my tears,

I watched you fly. Pleasant. Melodious. Soft. Everything I wasn't. Everything you invited me to be. Each beat of your wings was a new spark, reminding me of everything I had learnt. The larva I used to be, the cocoon I had enclosed myself in and the wings I had grown. It was only when you performed your gentle acrobatics in the air and landed on my nose that I realised what I was doing with her wings: preventing them from flying. Perched between my eyes, you seemed to be watching, as if challenging me. My tears abated. My sobs came at longer intervals. I was coming back to you. I was coming back to me. I blinked and saw your wings follow my eyelids. When my eyelids dropped, they dropped with you. When my eyelids lifted again, they followed your upwards motion. That was it. While my eyes opened and closed and your wings beat, the breeze continued and we were part of it all. I became so aware of the movement of my eyelids that I remember having felt afraid at the thought of not seeing you again, every time they opened, after having closed against your image, in the fraction of a second it took. In the awareness of this fraction of time, there was an assurance of eternity: you were always there, each time I trusted myself to close my eyes, unsure of what I would see when I opened them. You might not be there, but my hope of seeing you again was there, fed by the certainty of memories that could be seen again and again, forever. I gave in to that fraction of a second again. My eyes closed. I trusted. I waited. I remembered. My eyes opened. You weren't there. But I could still see you. You were beautiful when you perched on me, but you were even more beautiful in flight. I'm grateful to you for teaching me. I wasn't prepared for a love like this, but your wisdom made up for the absence of mine. Suddenly aware, I got up and, gradually accelerating into a run, I went back to the place I never should have left. I hoped to see her. I hoped she hadn't already flown away.

'You came back?' I held her in an embrace that contained the possibility that it might be the last. 'Sorry.'

'I should be saying sorry to you, I shouldn't have hidden this from you.'

'That's true, but it doesn't justify my reaction. I want you to listen to me, because I don't know if I'll ever be able to say this if I don't do it now.' I took her hands. 'Thank you. Thank you for everything. For the company, for the closeness, for the affection, for the loyalty, for the lessons... for the love. For everything you've given me and for everything you showed me I can be. I'm terribly afraid of losing you, because I've got used to thinking that I can only be this way with you, but that wasn't what your love taught me. That's what fear has taught me. My childhood. My losses. Our losses: your empathy showed me that I was never alone, even when I didn't know you. Before I heard what you'd been through, you were there experiencing it and breaking through my solitude. We are never alone, if we remember the empathy that binds us to others. I learnt that with you.' Her eyes sparkled as she listened to me. The combination of

227

nostalgia and pride that shone out of them confirmed that I loved her in a way I had never been able to love before. 'Your love reminds me that, in the memory of our experiences and the hope that feeds the future, I will never lose you. I just want for you what you always wanted for me.' I paused. At that moment, I wasn't looking into her eyes. I was looking into her soul. 'I don't want you to crawl for me. I don't want you to protect yourself from me. I want you to fly. As high as you can go, cradled by the wind, the way you reminded me to be. I don't know if you were the love of my life, but you were certainly the love that changed my life. I will never forget you, because you taught me never to forget myself. I hope that I am now doing the same for you: fly. You're beautiful perching on me, but you're even more beautiful in flight.' She kissed me. My wings trembled. I had forgotten I had them, until I accepted that she could use hers. Until I encouraged her to do it. In the act of letting ourselves fly, we must beat our own wings. She flew. I was just beginning.

We made the most of each day that followed, until she departed on the journey that would take her to her dreams. At first it was hard without her, but the echo of her lessons remained: it wasn't love that made me suffer, it was the pain of loss. Feeling it was a part, but it wasn't the whole. I never again confused the concepts, even though I experienced them at other stages in life. I told her about all these experiences in the letters we exchanged. Knowing she was happy made me happy and that relieved the yearning. If she was able to visit me, she did.

If I was able to visit her, I did. But never with any kind of obligation or expectation. We were committed to the constant appreciation of our own flight. That's how it was until the end. That's how it was, until now.

I have in my hands the last letter she sent me after coming to visit to say goodbye. She knew that it would be the last time she saw me, in this life. My health, compatible with my age, left no room for illusion. It was good to see her again for the last time and remember that, in life, once is enough to know what love is. I re-read the last paragraph she wrote to me. I use her words the way I became accustomed to using her very existence: as a source of inspiration. 'Do you remember when you helped me to fly and you remembered that you had wings? Well, now the time has come to use them fully and embrace the next transformation. Don't be afraid. Life has prepared you for this moment and taught you that, in love, the next transformation is always for the better. Even when we can't see what is coming. It's no coincidence that the word metamorphosis has 'more' in the middle. Every change is a chance for more. More love. More trust. Love until the end and I promise to love you beyond that. That way, the end will never come.'

I place the letter on my chest. Open, so that the world can see the love I found. I'm lying down, surrounded by the walls of the room where I spent so much time working, more importantly the room where I got to know her. It smells of lime. Outside the window is the tree she taught me to see as the breeze that goes beyond our last breath.

The warmth of the sun fills my body and the light surrounds me in a never-ending kiss that invites me to sleep without fear. And here you are, watching me. I smile. I knew you wouldn't let me down at this moment. I watch you with the certainty of an imminent goodbye. The first one I accept without pain. I see, in the corner, on the table where I ate my last meal, some memories that I once thought about disposing of. They too went through their metamorphosis and turned into something now worth remembering. In the lunch box, I now keep more than the sound of that engine. And on the tablecloth, the crumbs of a fragmented love that, now, I feel in its entirety. In a place of pain, there is always the possibility of a place of love. You are perched on the windowsill. The same light that lands on me shines through your wings. Life blows gently through them. Yours. Mine. Ours. We are, in the end, ready to fly.

I lived for the first time when I learnt that to love is to let go.

ABOUT THIS STORY

'Three Steps to Learn How to Fly' is a collective work, produced and illustrated by two Year 12 classes from **Cacilhas Secondary School** (Almada, Portugal) under the guidance of writer **André Fernandes** between November 2018 and January 2019.

Participating pupils: **Alexandra Montez, Ana Cecília Rodrigues, Ana Rita Faia, Beatriz Cardoso, Carolina Mendes, Cátia Baptista, Daniela Conceição, Diogo Arjones, Érica Nambua, Gabriel Gea Martins, Inês Flores Silva, Inês Tatiana Marques, Joana Maria Barroso, Márcia Sofia Capelas, Margarida Rodrigues, Mariana Pires, Marta Caramelo, Nicole Castanho, Núria Pegudo, Pedro Rebocho, Raquel Ribeiro, Tiago Afonso, Vinicius Souza, Joana Gramaça, Rebecca Carvalho, Ângela Maria Silva, Beatriz Palmeirim, Ester Tinoco Serra, Eva Pinho Guerreiro, Gabriela Horta, Inês Silva Lopes, Lara Sofia Praça, Mafalda Figueiredo, Marcelo Tavares, Margarida Rey Costa, Maria Ourives Pratas, Mariana Purificação, Vitória São Pedro, Filipe Carrilho, Gonçalo Santos** and **Joana Bastos**.

ABOUT THE WRITER

André Fernandes was born in 1991 in Lisbon. He graduated at the age of 21 from the Faculty of Social Sciences at Universidade Nova de Lisboa with a degree in Communication Sciences, in the field of Journalism and Cinema/TV. A year later, he published his first work, 'Aunt Guida,' which told of his experiences living with his Aunt Margarida at a time when she was facing terminal cancer. At the age of 25, he launched his second literary project: '25+ Life is a School,' in which he shares the most important life lessons learnt during his first quarter of a century, reflecting on professional fulfilment, bullying and spirituality, among many other themes.

ABOUT THE TRANSLATORS

Nancy Langfeldt is a British/Norwegian literary translator. She moved to the UK to study Engish Literature at the University of York and has remained here since, making Birmingham home for the past ten years. In 2015 Nancy completed a mentorship under translator Don Bartlett through the British Institure of Literary Translation. In addition to translating she works at Loaf Community Bakery and Birmingham Bike Foundry, two worker co-operatives in the city.

Beth Fowler was born in 1980, in Inverness. She studied Hispanic Studies at the University of Glasgow, spending time in Chile and Portugal as part of her course. She has been a translator since 2009, working from Portuguese and Spanish to English. In 2010, she won the Harvill Secker Young Translators' Prize and shortly afterwards was commissioned to do her first book-length translation, *Open Door*, by Iosi Havilio (And Other Stories, 2011). Since then she has had a further three novel translations published: *Paradises,* also by Iosi Havilio (And Other Stories, 2013), *Ten Women*, by Marcela Serrano (Amazon Crossing, 2014) and *We All Loved Cowboys*, by Carol Bensimon (Transit Books, 2018). She lives near Glasgow with her husband and two children.

ABOUT THE ILLUSTRATOR

Riya Chowdhury is an illustrator based in the West Midlands who likes to experiment with different mediums, including traditional and digital. She is interested in fantasy and science fiction themes but likes to challenge her skills and work outside of her comfort zone.

See more of her work here: www.ri-ya.co.uk

Spark
Young Writers

Creative writing groups
for children and
young people in the
West Midlands

£63 per year
£7 per session
Aged 8 - 17

www.writingwestmidlands.org